Her knees went weak.

It happened whenever she looked at him. "I'm sorry I've been angry with you all these years. You were wrong, but…" Her throat constricted as she remembered. But maybe she'd rushed things. They were hardly out of their teens when she'd realized she loved him. And now…

"I think you'd better go," she managed.

He stood. "I'll be back tomorrow."

"To work on the house?"

"To work on the house. And to court you."

"That's why the matchmaker brought you here, isn't it? That was your plan from the beginning."

"*Ya*, I hoped she could help me get my foot in the door," he admitted. "But this, now, is about you and me. Let me show you I'm not the boy I was nine years ago."

"And I'm not the girl."

He grabbed his coat and hat. "We could make a good couple."

She remained seated. Her legs were too wobbly to stand. "I can't promise anything, Luke."

"But you'll think about it?"

She'd think about it…but she couldn't guess what her answer would be.

Emma Miller lives quietly in her old farmhouse in rural Delaware. Fortunate enough to be born into a family of strong faith, she grew up on a dairy farm, surrounded by loving parents, siblings, grandparents, aunts, uncles and cousins. Emma was educated in local schools and once taught in an Amish schoolhouse. When she's not caring for her large family, reading and writing are her favorite pastimes.

Visit the Author Profile page at Harlequin.com for more titles.

A Man for Honor

Emma Miller

HARLEQUIN® LOVE INSPIRED®

Recycling programs
for this product may
not exist in your area.

 LOVE INSPIRED BOOKS

ISBN-13: 978-1-335-50928-4

A Man for Honor

www.Harlequin.com

Printed in U.S.A.

Then came Peter to him, and said, Lord,
how oft shall my brother sin against me,
and I forgive him? till seven times? Jesus saith
unto him, I say not unto thee, Until seven times:
but, Until seventy times seven.
—*Matthew* 18:21–22

Chapter One

Luke Weaver lifted the collar of his lined jean jacket to his neck, pulled down his still-wet black hat and made his way toward the exit of the convenience store and the raw December morning.

"That *is* you, isn't it?" the college-aged boy behind the register called after Luke. He pointed to the TV screen mounted above the snacks section. "Look!" he proclaimed to several customers. "That guy's the mystery cowboy they're looking for! He's the hero that rescued those people from the bus wreck in Pennsylvania last night!"

Luke kept walking. The last thing he wanted was to be recognized in his hometown of Dover, Delaware. When a tractor trailer had skidded on an icy highway the previous night, causing a multivehicle collision, he'd been in the midst of it. The bus he'd been riding had flipped on its side and slid down an embankment into a deep drainage pond. With icy water fast pouring in and people panicking, he hadn't considered that his photo might end up being plastered all over the national news.

Luke had acted without thinking. He'd pulled the

unconscious driver to safety and then broken a window to assist a mother and several small children out of the sinking bus. He'd gone back into the rapidly submerging vehicle twice to help other trapped passengers before state troopers and paramedics arrived. One of the officers had asked who he was, but not wanting to draw attention to himself, he'd refused to give his name. And that had only made things worse because the news media had made a big thing of it. Now everyone was hunting for the *mystery cowboy*, calling him a real-life superhero.

"Hey, mister! Are you the super cowboy?" a woman headed toward the doors to the convenience store asked as he stepped out. "You look just like him."

Luke strode down Lepore Street. He was supposed to meet someone from the Seven Poplars Amish community at the bus stop, but he wasn't hanging around. He'd find his own way to Sara Yoder's home.

Beads of freezing sleet stung his face and hands, but he kept walking. Winters in Delaware weren't as cold as those in Kansas, and he could dry off when he got to the matchmaker's. He hoped someone had some spare clothes he could change into, because the trousers he was wearing were ripped and stained, and his duffle bag with spare clothes was still in the bus's luggage compartment, probably resting at the bottom of that drainage pond.

Luke had just crossed the street and turned onto North State when he caught sight of a mule and buggy coming at a sharp pace. Guessing that that must be his ride, he waved the driver to a stop. To his surprise, the only occupant of the buggy was a plump, middle-aged Amish woman with dark curly hair, a nutmeg-colored complexion, and eyes as dark and shiny as ripe black-berries. "Sara?"

She nodded. "You must be Luke," she said in *Deitsch* and then switched to English. "Jump in before we cause a traffic jam."

He glanced up and down the street. Not a single vehicle was coming in either direction. He looked back at Sara as he swung up onto the bench seat. The interior of the buggy was plain black, neat and well maintained, pretty much what he'd expected of the woman he only knew from correspondence. "Dover hasn't grown all that much in the time I've been gone," he said.

"*Atch.* According to my neighbors, it *has* grown. They say the traffic has increased," she replied. "I moved here from a rural area of Wisconsin a few years back, so Kent County still seems busy to me. You're certain you want to trade the wide-open spaces of the Midwest for our little state?"

He nodded. "*Ya*, I do."

"You said in your first letter that you grew up here."

"I did, and I've always thought of Kent County as home," he answered. "Kansas can be pretty dry. I miss the green and the rain."

A line of cars slowed behind them, but Sara didn't seem to notice. "Rain we have aplenty," she said after a bit.

"And a strong church community." He stretched out his long legs and rubbed absently at his aching shoulder. When the collision happened, he'd been thrown violently against the corner of the seat frame across the aisle. Nothing seemed broken, but he guessed he was going to have quite a bruise. "At least, that's the way I remember it," he finished.

"It is. And everyone will welcome you. We're always glad to add to our family. You say you're a master carpenter?"

"More of a cabinetmaker, but I can do any type of construction."

Sara looked at him with frank curiosity. "I'm curious as to why you'd need my services. A nice-looking man like you with a good trade? Back in Kansas, mothers must have been parading their daughters in front of you. Girls must have been lining up hoping you'd take them home from a singing."

But not the woman I want, he thought. To Sara, he said, "I'm ready to marry and start a family, but I thought the whole process would be easier if I used a matchmaker."

"Mmm." Sara's brow arched. "I've checked up on you. Wrote a couple of letters. Your bishop tells me that you're baptized and a solid member of your church." She pursed her lips. "A matchmaker can certainly make it easier finding the right wife, but why me? Why not someone in Kansas?"

"The nearest Amish matchmaker to where I lived just celebrated her eighty-second birthday, and she doesn't hear or see well. Besides, I want to move back to Delaware and marry a woman from here." He glanced at her. "You have a good reputation. People speak of you as one of the best, and you specialize in hard-to-place cases."

Her eyes narrowed. "Are you a difficult case, Luke Weaver?" She gave him an appraising look. "I'll admit you do look a little worse for wear."

"Ya." He ran a hand over the three-cornered tear in the knee of his go-to-church trousers. There was a stain on the other leg he suspected might be blood and

his wide-brimmed black wool hat had taken a beating. The brim was sagging and it was shrinking as it dried; it wasn't meant to be submerged in water.

"I suppose I do," he admitted. He considered whether or not to explain his condition to Sara. His first impressions of her were good, but he didn't know that he was ready to tell anyone what had happened on the highway the previous night. The idea of talking about it made him uncomfortable; he'd done what any man would have done. End of story.

Sara turned off State Street onto Division. Traffic was still light for the center of town. A few pedestrians stopped and watched as the mule and buggy passed. A little boy in a fire-engine red rain slicker and yellow boots waved from the sidewalk, and Sara waved back.

"A lot of new construction in Dover," he commented as the grand Victorian houses gave way to commercial buildings and smaller frame homes. "I'm hoping I'll be able to find steady employment."

"There's always work for a carpenter," she replied. "A good friend of mine has a construction crew. You'll meet him at church tomorrow." Her shrewd gaze raked him again. "If you're planning on joining us for worship. It's being held at Samuel Mast's, not far from my place. You know Samuel?"

"I do. Good man. And *ya*, I do want to attend service. If you can find me something decent to wear. We, um… had some trouble… The bus." He cleared his throat. "I'm afraid my duffle bag with all my clothes is lost. I don't want to impose. I know I've picked an awkward time to arrive, two days after Christmas, but…it was time I came."

"Not a problem. I can find clothes, and I've got a

warm bed for you. All my prospective brides have either married or gone back to their families for the holidays. It's much too quiet in my house. Even our little school-teacher has gone visiting relatives. As I told you in my letter, I have a bunkhouse for my hired hand and male clients from out of state. Some stay for the weekend, others a few weeks or longer. It's far enough from the house for propriety, but close enough so that your meals won't be cold before you get to the table. Prospective brides stay in the house with me."

"The bunkhouse sounds great. I appreciate it," he said. "And I appreciate you coming to get me. It's a miserable day for you to be on the road."

Sara reined the mule to a stop as the light ahead turned from yellow to red. "I could have sent Hiram for you. He's my hired man. But his judgment's not the best. He might have decided to take the buggy down the DuPont Highway to stop at the mall. And the mad-house of a highway is no place for a mule, even a sen-sible one." She glanced at Luke. "And the truth is, I was looking for an excuse to get out of the house."

They rode in comfortable silence for a few minutes and then Luke spoke up again. He wasn't one to keep quiet on things. Sometimes he was criticized for speak-ing too easily from his heart, with his feelings. It wasn't something necessarily encouraged in Amish men, but he was who he was. "I hope you're going to be able to help me make a match," he said. If she couldn't, he didn't know what he'd do.

"No reason why I shouldn't, is there?" She glanced at him again. "I'll admit, Luke, you are something of a mystery to me. You do make me curious."

He winced at the word *mystery* but said nothing.

"You know, young women seeking husbands are plentiful, but eligible bachelors with a solid trade seeking brides aren't as easy to find. From what I see with my eyes, and from what I've learned from your letters and my own inquiries, you're almost too good to be true."

"I don't know about that. I'm as flawed as any man. But I assure you, I've not told you any untruths."

"I didn't say you had," Sara said. "My first thought would be that I can think of a good dozen young women who would jump at the opportunity to meet you. But something tells me that there's more to you, that you've not told me everything I need to know if I'm going to make the right match for you."

He grimaced. "There is something I haven't said."

"And that is?"

"There's a particular someone I've set my mind on, someone special I used to know." He stopped and started again. "Someone I haven't been able to forget."

Sara reined the mule off the street and into a parking place in a car dealership lot. She looped the leathers over a hook on the dash, folded her arms and turned to face him. "I take it that this *someone* is of legal age, Amish and free to marry?"

"She is."

"But you didn't think that I should have that information before you arrived?"

He tugged on the sagging brim of his hat. It was a shame it was ruined because he'd bought it new before he left Kansas. "I thought it would be easier if I could explain in person." He looked away and then back at the matchmaker. "Her name is Honor. Honor King."

Sara didn't hide her surprise. "I know Honor. A

widow. She doesn't belong to our church community, but I have introduced her to several prospects. Honor's husband passed a year and a half ago."

"Nineteen months."

Sara frowned. "And you know that Honor has children. Four of them."

"*Ya*, I do. That doesn't matter to me."

"Well, it should," she harrumphed. "It takes a special kind of a man to be a father to another man's children. Especially as they get up in age."

He felt himself flush. "I know that. What I said about the children, that didn't come out right. Her children are part of her. I want to be a good father to them. And a good husband to her."

Sara raised a dark eyebrow. "You're familiar with Honor's children? You've met them?"

There was something in her tone that made him hesitate. "*Ne*...but I hope to have many children."

She sniffed. "Easily said by a man who has none. As the preachers tell us, children are blessings from God. That said, they can be a handful. Some more than others." She pursed her lips. "Any other revelations you'd like to share with me?"

He hesitated. "Well..."

"Like this, perhaps?" She reached under the seat and came up with a copy of the *Delaware State News*. The photo snapped by one of the bus passengers stared back at him. It was clearly his face, with a fire truck and a Pennsylvania State Police car in the background. In his arms was a screaming child. Under the photo, a bold headline proclaimed Mystery Cowboy Rides to the Rescue!

"You saw it," he said.

"*Ya*, saw it and read it. What I didn't know was that I would be welcoming the mystery cowboy into my home. You know our community takes a dim view of photographs. They are forbidden."

"In my church, as well," he agreed. "But I didn't give anyone permission to take a picture. And I didn't ask for people to talk about what happened. There was an accident. I did what seemed right."

"But it will make talk." She allowed herself the hint of a smile. "A lot of talk."

"I was afraid of that."

"That the hat you were wearing?" She frowned, looking up at him. "Doesn't look much like a *gunslinger's* hat. Or a rodeo rider's."

"*Ne.*"

She had a sense of humor, this perky little matchmaker. He liked her. Better yet, he had the strongest feeling that he could trust her in what might be the biggest step of his life.

Sara chuckled. "*Englishers.* Mistook your church hat for a cowboy hat, I suppose, and thought you were a cowboy."

"*Ya.* Someone who isn't familiar with our people."

She nodded. "I can see that. Better for you that it doesn't say *Amish*. Better for us."

"Maybe so," he said.

"I know so." Her eyes lit with mischief. "But good of you to save the *Englishers* from the accident. They are God's children, too."

"I didn't want the fuss. Anybody would have done what I did."

"But according to the newspaper, you're the one who took charge. Who kept his head, did what needed to be done and kept the unconscious bus driver from drowning. Not everyone would have the courage to do that." She paused and then went on. "There'll be questions we'll have to answer from our neighbors, but if you don't wear snakeskin boots, rope cows or sign autographs, the talk will pass and people will find something else to gossip about."

"I hope so."

She reached over and patted his arm reassuringly. "If you didn't want your photograph taken, there's no reason to feel guilty about it. Any of our people with sense will come to realize it." She gathered the reins again and clicked to the mule. And as they pulled out onto the street again, she said, "One question for you. The widow, Honor King, will she look favorably on your suit?"

"I doubt it," he admitted, gazing out at the road ahead. "She returns my letters unopened."

Two days later, Luke and Sara drove west from her house in Seven Poplars. Eventually, they passed a millpond and mill, and then went another two miles down a winding country road to a farm that sat far back off the blacktop.

"I don't know what her husband, Silas, was thinking to buy so far from other Amish families," Sara mused. "I haven't been here to Honor's home, because she lives out of our church district, but Freeman and Katie at the mill are her nearest Amish neighbors. It must be difficult for Honor since her husband passed away, being so isolated." She turned her mule into the driveway. *"Atch,"* she muttered. "Look at this mud. I hope we don't get stuck in the ruts." The lane, lined on either side by sagging fence rails and overgrown barbed wire, was filled with puddles.

"If we do, I'll dig us out," Luke promised, adjusting the shrunken hat that barely fitted on his head anymore. Now that they were almost to Honor's home, he was nervous. What if she refused to let him walk through her doorway? What if he'd sold everything he owned, turned his life upside down and moved to Delaware just to find that she'd have nothing to do with him?

Honor's farmhouse was a rambling, two-story frame structure with tall brick chimneys at either end. Behind and to the sides, loomed several barns, sheds and outbuildings. A derelict windmill, missing more than half its blades, leaned precariously over the narrow entrance to the farmyard.

"I'd have to agree with what you told me yesterday, Sara. She needs a handyman," Luke said, sliding his door open so he could get a better look. He'd heard that Honor's husband had purchased a big farm in western Kent County, near the Maryland state line. But no one had told him that the property was in such bad shape.

How could a woman alone with four children possibly manage such a farm? How could she care for her family? Why had Silas brought his young bride here? Fixing up this place would have been a huge undertaking for a healthy man, not to mention one who'd suffered from a chronic disease since he was born.

The wind shifted and the intermittent rain dampened Luke's trousers and wet his face. He pulled the brim of his hat low to shield his eyes as the mule plodded on up the drive, laying her ears back against the rain and splashing through the puddles. As the buggy neared the farmhouse, Luke noticed missing shingles on the roof and a broken window on the second floor. His chest tightened and he felt an overwhelming need to do whatever he could to help Honor, regardless of how she received him.

As they passed between the gateposts that marked the entrance to the farmyard, Luke could hear the rusty mechanism of the windmill creak and grind. The gate, or what remained of it, sagged, one end on the ground and overgrown with weeds and what looked like poison ivy.

"If I'd known things were this bad here, I would have asked Caleb to organize a work frolic to clean this place up," Sara observed. "Caleb's our young preacher, married one of the Yoder girls. You know Hannah Yoder? Her daughters are all married now, have families of their own."

"Knew Jonas Yoder well. He was good to me when I was growing up."

"Jonas was like that," Sara mused. "Hannah and I are cousins."

Luke continued to study the farm. "You've never been here before?"

"*Ne*, I haven't. She's been to my place, though. I'd heard Honor doesn't have church services here, but I always assumed it was due to Silas's illness and then her struggle to carry on without him."

Luke didn't know how long Honor's husband had been sick before he'd been carried off by a bout of pneumonia, but either he'd been sick a long time or he hadn't attended to his duties. The state of things on this farm was a disgrace.

A child's shriek caught his attention, and he glanced at the barn where a hayloft door hung open. Suddenly, a squirming bundle of energy cannonballed out of the loft, landed on a hay wagon heaped with wet straw and then vaulted off to land with a squeal of laughter in a mud puddle. Water splashed, ducks and chickens flew, squawking and quacking, in every direction, and a miniature donkey shied away from the building and added a shrill braying to the uproar.

The small figure climbed out of the puddle and shouted to someone in the loft. Luke thought the muddy creature must be a boy, because he was wearing trousers and a shirt, but couldn't make out his face or the color of his hair because it was covered in mud.

"What are you doing?" Sara called to the child. "Does your mother know—"

She didn't get to finish her sentence because a second squealing child leaped from the loft opening. He hit the heap of straw in the wagon and landed in the puddle with a satisfying splash and an even louder protest from the donkey. This child was shirtless and wearing only one shoe. When a third child appeared in the loft, this one the smallest of the three, Luke managed to leap out of the buggy and get to the wagon in time to catch him in midair.

This little one, in a baby's gown, was bareheaded, with clumps of bright red-orange hair standing up like the bristles on a horse's mane and oversize boots on the wrong feet. The rescued toddler began to wail. With a yell, the shirtless boy launched himself at Luke, fists and feet flying, and bit his knee.

"Let go of him!" the leader of the pack screamed in *Deitsch.* "*Mam!* A man is taking Elijah!"

Luke deposited Elijah safely on the ground. "Stop that!" he ordered in *Deitsch*, lifting his attacker into the air and tucking him under one arm.

"What do you think you're doing?"

Luke turned toward the back porch. A young woman appeared, a crying baby in her arms, wet hair hanging loose around her shoulders. "Let go of my son this minute!"

For a moment Luke stood there, stunned, the boy still flailing against his arm. Luke had been expecting to see a changed Honor, one weighed down by the grief of widowhood and aged by the birth of four children in six years, but he hadn't been prepared for this bold beauty. He opened his mouth to answer, but as he did, a handful of mud struck him in the cheek.

"Put Justice down!" the biggest boy shouted as he scooped up a handful of mud and threw it at Luke. "You let my brother go!"

The little one did the same.

Luke spit mud and tried to wipe the muck out of his eyes, only succeeding in making it worse.

Sara, now out of the buggy, clapped her hands. "*Kinner!* Stop this at once! Inside with you. You'll catch your deaths of ague." She reached out for Justice, and Luke gladly handed him, still kicking and screaming, over to her.

Honor came down the steps, carefully stepping over a hole where a board was missing. "Sara? I didn't realize—" She broke off. "You?" she said to Luke, raising her voice. "You dare to come here?"

He sucked in a deep breath. "*Goot mariye*, Honor. I know you weren't expecting me, but—"

"But nothing," Honor flung back. Red-haired Elijah's cry became a shriek, and a dog ran out of the house and began to bark. Honor raised her voice further to be heard over the noise. "What are doing here, Luke?"

"Calm down," he soothed, raising both hands, palms

up, in an attempt to dampen the fire of her temper. "Hear me out, before—"

"There will be no *hearing you out*," she said, interrupting him again. "You're not welcome here, Luke Weaver."

"Now, Honor—"

"Why did you bring him here, Sara?" Honor demanded.

To add to the confusion, the rainfall suddenly became a downpour. Sara looked up at the dark sky and then at Honor. "If you've any charity, I think we'd best get under your roof before we all drown," she said.

Honor grimaced and reached out for the child struggling in Sara's arms. "Could you grab Elijah?" she asked the matchmaker. "Stop that, Justice," she said, balancing her middle child on one hip and the baby against her shoulder. "Why are you half-dressed? Where's Greta? And where's your coat?" She glanced up. "*Ya*, come in, all of you. Elijah! Tanner!" She rolled her eyes. "You, too, Luke. Although it would serve you right if I did leave you out here to drown."

Chapter Two

Honor set Justice down on the top step and herded him and the other two boys into the narrow passageway that served as a place to hang coats, wash clothing and store buckets, kindling and fifty other items she didn't want in her kitchen. "Watch your step," she warned Sara. "The cat had kittens, and they're constantly underfoot."

Her late husband had disliked cats in the house. The thought that this was her house and she could do as she pleased now, in spite of what he thought, gave her a small gratification in the midst of the constant turmoil. "Tanner? Where's Greta?" She glanced back at Sara who was setting Elijah on his feet. "Greta's Silas's niece. She helps me with the children and the housework." She raised her free hand in a hopeless gesture. "She was supposed to be checking on the sheep. She must have taken the little ones outside with her."

Kittens, sheep, Greta and the condition of her kitchen were easier for Honor to think about than Luke Weaver. She couldn't focus on him right now. Barely could imagine him back in Kent County, let alone in her house. What had possessed Sara to bring him here?

Queasiness coiled in the pit of Honor's stomach and made her throat tighten. It had taken her years to put Luke in her past…to try to forget him. And how many hours had she prayed to forgive him? That was still a work in progress. But she wouldn't let him upset her life. Not now. Not ever again. And yet, here he was in her home. *God, give me the strength*, she pleaded silently.

Confusion reigned in the damp laundry room where the ceiling sagged and the single window was cracked and leaked air around the rotting frame. Her baby daughter, Anke, began to wail again, and Justice was whining.

"Inside," Honor ordered, pointing. "You'll have to forgive the state of the house," she said over her shoulder to Sara. She chose to ignore Luke as she led the way into the kitchen. "The roof has a leak. Leaks." Her cheeks burned with embarrassment. Water dripped from the ceiling into an assortment of buckets and containers. Not that she had to tell Sara that the roof leaked. She could see it for herself. She could hear the cascade of falling drops.

Honor gazed around the kitchen, seeing it as her visitors must, a high-ceilinged room with exposed beams overhead, a bricked-up fireplace and cupboards with sagging doors. She'd painted the room a pale lemon yellow, polished the windowpanes until they shone and done her best with the patchy, cracked linoleum floor, but it was plain that soap and elbow grease did little against forty years of neglect. What must Sara think of her? As for Luke, she told herself that she didn't care what he thought.

But she did.

"Tanner," Honor said brusquely. "Take your brothers

to the bathroom. Greta will give you all a bath and clean clothes. As soon as I find her," she added. "But you've not heard the end of this," she warned, shaking a finger. It was an empty threat. She knew it and the children did, too, but it seemed like something a mother should say. She put the baby into her play yard and looked around. Where was that girl? Greta, sixteen, was not nearly as much help as Honor had hoped she would be when she'd agreed to have the girl come live with her. Sometimes, Honor felt as if Greta was just another child to tend to. "Tanner, where is Greta?"

Tanner flushed and suddenly took a great interest in a tear in the linoleum between his feet.

Justice piped up. "Feed room."

Tanner lifted his head to glare at his brother.

"What did you say?" Honor asked.

"Feed room." Justice clapped his hands over his mouth and giggled.

"What's she doing in the feed room?" Honor frowned, fearing the answer as she spoke.

Justice shrugged. "Can't get out." He cast a knowing look at his older brother, Tanner, whose face was growing redder by the second.

Honor brought the heel of her hand to her forehead. "Did you lock her in again?"

Tanner's blue eyes widened as he pointed at Elijah. "Not me. He did it."

"And you let him? Shame on you. You're the big boy. You're supposed to—"

"Wait, someone's locked in the feed room?" Luke interrupted, using his handkerchief to wipe the splatters of mud off his face.

"Tanner, you go this minute and let Greta out,"

Honor ordered, still ignoring the fact that Luke, *her* Luke, was standing in her kitchen. "And the three of you are in big trouble. There will be no apple pie for any of you tonight."

"I'll go," Luke offered, shoving his handkerchief into the pants he'd borrowed from Sara's hired hand. "Where's the feed room?"

"Barn," Tanner supplied.

"The'th in the barn," Elijah lisped.

Luke turned back toward the outer door.

Honor watched him go. The way it was pouring rain, he'd get soaked. She didn't care. She turned back to her boys. "Upstairs!" she said. "Go find dry clothes. Now. I'll send Greta up to run your bath. And you haven't heard the last of this. I promise you that."

They ran.

Honor exhaled and glanced at Sara. "I'm not as terrible a mother as I must seem. I was changing Anke's diaper. I thought Elijah was in his bed napping and the other two playing upstairs. Fully dressed. They *were* dressed the last time I saw them." She pressed her hand to her forehead again. "Really, they were."

Sara looked around the kitchen. She didn't have to say anything. Honor wanted to sink through the floor. Not that her kitchen was dirty. It wasn't, except that she'd been making bread. Who wouldn't scatter a little flour on the counter or floor? There were no dirty dishes in the sink, no sour diaper smell, and if her boys looked like muddy scarecrows, at least the baby was clean and neat. But the buckets all over the room…

"I hired someone to fix the roof and make the repairs to the house," Honor explained. "But—" She gave a wave. "It's a long story, but basically, it won't be happening anytime soon."

"I know," Sara supplied. "I heard. Robert Swartzentruber fell off a ladder and broke his ankle. A pity."

"*Ya*, a pity. Poor man. I've been looking for a replacement, but—" she opened her arms "—I've been a little busy."

"Which is exactly why I brought Luke Weaver," Sara said smoothly.

Honor studied her. Did Sara know about her and Luke? She *must* know. But it had all happened before Sara came to Seven Poplars. Maybe she didn't know. "Why him?" she asked.

"He's a master carpenter. And he's new to town and looking for work."

"I'm sorry. No, that's not possible." Honor picked up a small tree branch, brought in by one of her boys, and tossed it in the trash can. She checked her tone before she spoke again, because she'd been accused more than once of speaking too sharply to people. Of having too strong an opinion. "Luke Weaver is not working on my house," she declared. "I don't want him here. He's the last carpenter I'd—"

"Honor." Sara cut her off. "Think of your children. If you have a leak in the kitchen, you must have them elsewhere in the house. And your back step is broken. And you've got a cracked windowpane in your laundry room and another on the second floor. And the bad winter weather hasn't even set in on us."

"Half the house is broken," Honor answered honestly. Her late husband had bought the farm without her ever seeing the place. He'd promised to fix it up, but he hadn't kept many promises. And now she was left to deal with it.

"Don't let pride or an old disagreement keep you from doing what's best for your children," Sara cautioned.

So she knew *something*. The question was, what had he told her? "Just not him," Honor repeated. "Anyone else. I can pay. I don't need…" It was difficult to keep from raising her voice. Sara didn't understand. Couldn't understand. Honor didn't need Luke. Couldn't have him here. Why would he ever believe she would let him walk in and then hire him?

"I'm not asking you to marry him," Sara said with an amused look. "I know you have a history—"

"A *history*?" Honor flared, feeling her cheeks grow warm. "Is *that* what he told you?"

"The details aren't my business." Sara's face softened. "Honor, I know how difficult it can be for a widow alone. I've been there. But you have to make choices that are in your best interest. And those of your children. If Luke's willing to make the repairs you need and you pay a fair wage, you're not obligated to him. He's an employee, nothing more. He could do the job and then move on. And you and your children would be much better off."

Honor shook her head. The insides of her eyelids stung and she could feel the emotions building up inside her, but she wouldn't cry. There was no way Luke would make her cry again. "He didn't tell you what he did to me, did he?"

"He wanted to, but I wouldn't hear of it," Sara said. "As I said, I don't need to know. What I do know is that he seems to be a good man."

"I believed that, too. Once, a long time ago." Honor gripped the back of a chair. "But then he walked out on me nine years ago." Against her will, tears filled her eyes. "The morning we were to be married."

As soon as Luke walked into the barn, he could tell where the feed room was by the muffled shouts and thuds. He found his way past a dappled gray horse, a placid Jersey cow, stray hens and a pen of sheep to a door with a wooden bar across it. He swung the bar up, and the door burst open. Out spilled a slight, sandy-haired, teenage girl with tear-streaked cheeks.

"They locked me in again!" she declared. She seemed about to elaborate on her plight when she suddenly saw him and stopped short in her tracks, eyes wide. *"Atch!"* she cried and clapped a hand over her mouth.

"I'm Luke," he said. "Honor sent me to let you out." That wasn't exactly true, but close enough without going into a detailed explanation. "Are you all right?"

"They are bad children! Bad!" she flung back without answering his question. "And that oldest is the worst. Every day, they lock me in the feed room." She thrust out her lower lip, sniffed and began to weep again. "I want to go home."

"Don't cry," Luke said. "You say they lock you in the feed room every day? So why…why did you give them the opportunity to lock you in? Again and again?"

"Aagschmiert. Tricked. I was tricked." She wiped her nose with the back of the sleeve of her oversize barn coat. "And it's dark in there. I hate the dark."

"Ya." Luke nodded. "I'm not overly fond of it myself. At least I wouldn't be if someone locked me in."

He reached out and removed a large spiderweb from the girl's headscarf.

She shuddered when she saw it. *"Wildheet,"* she insisted. "Wild, bad *kinner.*" She pointed at a chicken. "See? They let the chickens out of their pen, too. And yesterday it was the cow. Everything, they let loose. Me, they lock in."

Luke pressed his lips tightly together and tried not to laugh. "As I said, I'm Luke. I came to make repairs to the house. And who are you?"

"Greta. Silas's niece. From Ohio." Another tear rolled down her cheek. "But going home, I think. Soon."

"Well, Greta from Ohio, best we get back in the house before they send someone else out in the rain to see if I'm locked up somewhere, too."

Still muttering under her breath about bad children, Greta led the way through the cluttered barn and, hunching her back against the downpour, made a dash for the house.

They went inside, leaving their wet coats and his hat hanging on hooks in the laundry room, and made a beeline for the woodstove in the kitchen. Greta's teeth were chattering. Luke had the shivers, but he clamped his teeth together and refused to give in to the chill. He put his hands out to the radiating heat, grateful for the semidry kitchen, and glanced sideways at Honor.

In the time since he'd gone to the barn and returned, she'd twisted up her hair and covered it with a woolen scarf. Her plain blue dress had seen better days and her apron was streaked with flour and mud. Her black wool stockings were faded; her slender feet were laced into high black leather shoes. Honor had always been a small woman, and now she was even more slender and more graceful. Life and motherhood had pared away the girlish roundness of her face, leaving her stunning to his eye, more beautiful than he'd dreamed.

"Again?" she said to the girl. "You let them lock you in *again*?"

Greta began to sniffle.

"None of that," Honor said, not unkindly. "Go change into dry things and then find the boys. They need a bath and clean clothes."

"The wash is still damp," Greta protested. "I hung it in the attic like you said, but it's still wet."

"Then bathe them and put them into their nightshirts. I won't have them running around the house in those muddy clothes."

"They won't listen to me," Greta muttered. "Justice won't get in the tub and the little one will run off as soon as I turn my back to him."

"Never you mind, child," Sara said. "I'll come along and lend a hand. I've bathed my share of unwilling *kinner*. And, I promise you, they won't get the best of me." She fixed Luke with a determined gaze. "Honor and Luke have some matters to discuss in private, anyway. Don't you?"

He nodded, feeling a little intimidated by Sara. She reminded him of his late mother.

"I wrote to you," he said when they were alone, as he held out his cold fingers to the warm woodstove. "I wrote every month since I heard that…that your husband passed. You refused my letters and they were returned." He searched her face, looking for some hint that she still cared for him…that she could forgive him. "I apologized for—"

"I didn't want to hear what you had to say then or now," she answered brusquely.

He exhaled. "Honor, I was wrong. I regret what I did, but I can't change the past." Only a few feet separated them. He wanted to go to her, to clasp her hands in his. But he didn't; he stood where he was. "I'm sorry, Honor. What more can I say?"

"That you'll go back to Kansas and leave me in peace."

"I can't do that." He gestured to the nearest leak in the ceiling. "You need help. And I'm here to do whatever you need. I'm a good carpenter. I can fix whatever's broken."

"Can you?" she asked softly.

And, for just a second, he saw moisture gleam in her large blue eyes. Emotion pricked the back of his throat. They weren't talking about the house anymore. They were talking about their hearts.

"I can try," he said softly.

She shook her head. "It's over, Luke. Whatever we had, whatever I felt for you, it's gone."

He stared at the floor. Despite her words, he still felt a connection to Honor. And he had a sense that what she was saying wasn't necessarily how she felt. So he took a leap of faith. He lifted his head to look into her eyes. "I'll be here first thing tomorrow morning with my tools. I know you hate me, but—"

"I don't hate you, Luke."

"Good, then we've a place to start. As I said, I'll be here early in the morning to start patching your roof."

"Patching won't do," she said, looking up and gesturing. "Look at this. The whole thing needs replacing."

"We'll see. If it can't be patched, I'll find a crew and we'll put on a new roof."

She faced him squarely, arms folded, chin up. "I want no favors from you."

"Then you'll have none. You can pay me whatever the going hourly wage is. I'll start in this kitchen and go from there. I'll mend whatever needs doing."

She pursed her lips, lips he'd once kissed and wanted desperately to kiss again. "You will, will you? And what if I lock the door on you?"

"You won't."

Darker blue clouds swirled in the depths of her beautiful eyes. "And what makes you so certain of that?"

"Because you'll think better of it. You didn't expect to see me here, and you're still angry. I get that. But you always had good sense, Honor. When you consider what's best for you and your children, you'll decide I'm the lesser of two evils."

"Which is?"

"Putting up with me doing your repairs is better than living with a leaky roof and a fallen windmill." He smiled at her. "And you will agree to let me do it. Because turning me away isn't smart, and you've always been the smartest woman I've ever known."

Chapter Three

Honor pulled back the curtain and peered out the kitchen window. *Maybe he won't come*, she told herself. *By this morning, he's realized he doesn't belong here. He'll give up and go back to Kansas. Go somewhere.* She certainly didn't want him here in Kent County. She didn't want to take the chance of running into him at Byler's Store or on the street in Dover. Luke Weaver was out of her life, and there was no way that she would ever let him back in again. She couldn't.

"Mam!" Elijah wailed. "My turn. My turn!"

"It's not!" Justice countered. "He went first. I want to feed the lamb. I want to feed—" with each word, her middle son's voice grew louder until he was shouting "—the lamb!"

"You already did. He did," Tanner said. "Besides, he's too little. They're both too little. It's my job to—"

"Please stop," Honor admonished as she turned away from the window, letting the curtain fall. It was foolish to keep looking for Luke. He wasn't coming. She didn't want him to come. She didn't know why was she looking for him. "I warned the three of you about fighting over the bottle." She crossed the kitchen and took the bottle out of Tanner's hands. "If you can't get along, none of you get to feed her. Go and wash your hands. *With soap.*"

The children scattered. The lamb bleated and wagged her stub of a tail. The old wooden playpen that had once confined her oldest son had been pressed into service as a temporary pen for the orphan lamb that had been silly enough to come into the world the previous night. It wasn't really an orphan, but the mother had refused to let it nurse, so it was either tend to it or see it die.

And the truth was that Honor had a soft spot for animals. She couldn't bear to see them in distress. She had to do whatever she could to save them. And the barn was too cold for a smaller-than-usual lamb with a careless mother. So it was added to the confusion that already reigned in her kitchen. It wasn't a good option, but she could think of no other.

Honor held the bottle at an angle, letting the lamb suck and wondering whether it would be possible to put a diaper on the fluffy animal. Probably not, she decided. She'd just have to change the straw bedding multiple times a day. At least here in her kitchen, near the woodstove, she wouldn't have to worry about keeping the little creature warm. And the rain had stopped, assuring that both animal and children wouldn't have to endure trickles of water dripping on their heads. "Thank You, God," she murmured.

There was a clatter of boots on the stairs and the three boys spilled into the kitchen again. "We're hungry," Tanner declared. He held up his damp hands to show that he'd washed.

Greta wandered into the room behind them, baby

Anke in her arms. Anke giggled and threw up her hands for Honor to take her.

"Just a minute, *kuche*," Honor said. "I have to finish giving the lamb her breakfast."

"I want breakfatht," Elijah reminded her.

Greta had made a huge batch of oatmeal earlier, but she'd burned it. It wasn't ruined, simply not pleasant. *Raisins and cinnamon could make it edible*, Honor supposed. But then she weakened. "I'll make you egg and biscuit," she offered.

"With scrapple," Justice urged. "Scrapple."

Justice liked to say the word. He didn't like scrapple, wouldn't eat meat of any kind, but the other boys did.

The other two took up the chant. "Scrapple, scrapple!"

Justice grinned. Sometimes, looking at him, Honor wondered just what would become of him when he was grown. He was a born mischief maker and unlikely to become a bishop. That was for certain.

The lamb drained the last of the formula from the bottle, butted her small head against the back of Honor's hand and kicked up her heels.

"She wants more," Tanner proclaimed, but Honor shook her head. Lambs, like children, often wanted to eat more than was good for them. She went to the sink and washed her hands, then looked around for a clean hand towel.

"All in the attic drying," Greta supplied. "Still wet."

Honor prayed for patience, dried her hands on her apron and turned on the flame under the cast-iron frying pan. "Get the eggs for me, will you, Greta?" she asked. That was a request she regretted a moment later when the girl stumbled, sending the egg carton flying out of her hand and bouncing off the back of a chair. Eggs splattered everywhere and the boys shrieked with excitement. Anke wailed.

Greta stood there and stared at the mess, looking as if she was about to burst into tears. "It was the cat's fault," she insisted. "Or maybe I slipped on a wet spot on the floor."

One remaining egg teetered on the edge of the table. Justice made a dive for it and missed. The egg rolled off. Tanner grabbed it in midair and the egg cracked between his fingers. The cat darted toward one of the broken eggs, only to be confronted by the dog. The cat hissed, and the dog began to bark, barely drowning out the shouts of the children.

"Clean it up, please," Honor told Greta. "And stop crying. It's only eggs." She scooped her daughter out of Greta's arms as a loud knock came at the back door. *"Ne,"* she muttered, closing her eyes for a moment. "It can't be." *Maybe it's someone from Sara's, come to tell me that Luke changed his mind*, she thought as she pushed open the back door.

But there he was, taller and handsomer than he'd seemed last night. He had just shaved; an Amish man didn't grow a beard until he married. She could smell the scent of his shaving cream. His blond hair, showing from beneath the too-small hat, was as yellow as June butter. She drew in a deep breath.

"Are you going to let me in?" he asked. And then that familiar grin started at the left corner of his mouth and spread, as sweet and slow as warm honey, across his face. "You look surprised to see me, Honor. I told you I'd be here."

Behind her, the kitchen chaos continued: Greta whin-

ing, the boys quarreling, the cat hissing at the dog and
the lamb bleating. For a few seconds, she felt as if she
were trapped in a block of ice. She couldn't let him in.
There was no way she could invite him into her house…
into her life. She'd lived through Luke Weaver once.
She could never do it again. She'd crack and break like
those eggs on the floor if she tried.

"Honor?" His green eyes seemed to dare her to turn
him away. Or were they daring her to let him in?

She turned and walked slowly back to the kitchen,
where the frying pan was smoking. Justice had pulled
off his shoes and was dancing barefoot in a mess of egg
yolk and crushed shell, and Elijah was trying to climb
into the lamb's playpen.

"Turn off the burner!" Honor called to Greta. "The
pan's too hot. There's smoke…" She trailed off and did
it herself.

Patience, she cautioned herself. If she wasn't gentle
with Greta, the girl would run weeping to her bed and
she'd be no help all the rest of the day. Not that she was
much help, but at least she was another pair of hands.
And there were never enough hands to do all that was
needed in the house or outside on the farm.

She thrust the baby into Greta's arms. "Put her in her
high chair and give her a biscuit. Break it up, or she'll
try to get it all in her mouth at once."

She realized that Justice and Tanner were staring
at something behind her. She glanced back and saw
that Luke had followed her into the kitchen. A leather
tool belt—weighed down with a carpenter's hammer,
screwdriver and pliers—was slung over one shoulder.
In his other hand he carried a metal toolbox. What was
he doing in here? She'd closed the door on him, hadn't

she? She opened her mouth to ask him what he thought he was doing, but clamped it shut just as quickly. She'd left the door open behind her…an invitation.

"Is that coffee I smell?" he asked.

"If you want some, pour it yourself. Cups are up there." She pointed to a line of mugs hanging on hooks.

"You remember that I like mine sweet." His tone was teasing.

"Cream is in the refrigerator. Sugar on the table." She turned her back on him, refusing to acknowledge his charm. She waved the smoke away from the stove.

"Honey?"

She snapped around, a hot retort ready to spring from her throat. But then she realized he was grinning at her and pointing to the plastic bee bottle on top of the refrigerator. Honey. Luke had always preferred honey in his coffee. She retrieved Elijah from the playpen, saving the lamb from certain destruction. *"Ne,"* she admonished. "You cannot ride her. She's not a pony."

"What if she was a pig?" Justice asked, leaning on the playpen. "You can ride a pig."

"You can't ride pigs!" Tanner corrected.

"Hungry," Elijah reminded her.

"Justice, put your boots on. The floor's cold."

"Once I fix those holes, it will be a lot warmer." Luke squirted honey into his coffee. "I need to get up on the roof now that the rain has passed. If it can't be patched, I'll have to look into getting a roofing crew together."

"Ask Freeman at the mill." Honor turned the flame on under the frying pan again and went to the refrigerator for scrapple. "Tanner, run out to the barn and see if you can find more eggs. Greta, go with him. You carry the eggs, and don't let him lock you in anywhere." She turned her gaze back to Luke. "James Hostetler has the best contracting bunch, but he's busy for months. I already tried him. If anyone is available and has the skill to hold a hammer, Freeman will know it."

"Freeman Kemp? I know him," he said, taking a seat at the table. "Did know him."

She turned her back on Luke again. She felt almost breathless with anger or something else, something she didn't want to confront. "*Ya,* Freeman owns the mill, so he's usually there."

"That's right. I forgot his family has the mill. I'll stop and talk with him on the way back to Sara's."

"If you're stopping there, you might as well pick up some chicken feed and save me the trip. I'll give you the money. That one can't drive a horse and wagon." She nodded in Greta's direction. "She's afraid of horses," she said, managing to keep any disapproval from her tone. She needed to work on judging people. But who ever heard of an Amish girl who was afraid of horses?

With the pan the right temperature, Honor added thick slices of scrapple. She tried to concentrate on what she was doing, because what sense would it make to burn herself making breakfast through foolishness over a man she'd put aside long ago? Rather, one who had put *her* aside. She winced inwardly. The hurt was still there, mended over with strong thread, almost forgotten, but still having the power to cause her pain if she dwelled on it.

"Good coffee," he remarked. "And that scrapple smells good, too. You always did have a steady hand at the stove."

She glanced over her shoulder and glared at him.

"No doubt Sara already fed you a substantial breakfast. She's known for her bountiful table."

Luke shrugged and offered that lethal grin of his. "I could eat a little something, if you're offering. A man can't do better than to start the day with a scrapple-and-egg biscuit."

"With catsup," Justice added. He carried a large bottle to the table and plopped it down in front of Luke. "I like catsup on my biscuit."

"That sounds good." Luke smiled at her son.

"That bottle's almost empty," Honor said. She was feeling a little steadier now. Children grounded a person. "Get *Mommi* another bottle from the pantry."

Justice darted off to get the catsup. Elijah climbed onto a chair and grabbed a biscuit from the plate on the table.

"Watch it doesn't burn." Luke pointed to Honor. "The scrapple."

She turned away from him and carefully turned the browning meat. "Your shoes are muddy," she said to Luke. "I'd appreciate it if you'd leave them in the laundry room. I scrubbed this floor once this morning."

Luke chuckled. "You've been busy. It's still early and you've made biscuits and mopped the floor and I don't know what else."

"Milked the cow and fed the livestock," Honor said, "and changed diapers and made beds. And if you don't take off those boots, I'll be scrubbing this floor again, too."

He got up from the table, went out of the room and removed his shoes. "Honor," he said as he returned in his stocking feet. His voice had lost the teasing note and become serious. "We need to talk. You know we need to talk about what happened, right?"

She shook her head. "*Ne*, I have nothing to say to you on that matter. It's long in the past. As for the present, do you want the job of fixing this house? If you do a decent job at a fair wage, I'll let you."

"You'll *let* me?"

She pressed her lips together. "I didn't ask you to come here."

"I couldn't stay away." He crossed the room to stand only an arm's length away from her. "You have to let me explain what happened. Why I did it."

She whirled around, hot spatula gripped in her hand, barely in control. *"Ne,"* she murmured. "I don't. I'll make use of your carpentry skills for the sake of my children. But there will be nothing more between us. Either you respect that, or you leave now."

His green eyes darkened with emotion.

Her breath caught in her throat.

"Honor," he said softly.

"*Ne*, Luke." She looked away. "You decide. Either we have a business arrangement or none at all."

"You know why I came back here."

His words gently nudged her, touching feelings she'd buried so long ago.

"Luke, I can't—"

The back door banged open and Tanner came flying in. "Eggs, *Mommi*. Lots of eggs. I found where the black hen had her nest."

"Good." Honor took a breath. "Wash your hands. Greta, put those eggs in the sink. Carefully." She laid the spatula on the table and clapped her hands. "Breakfast will be ready in two shakes of the lamb's tail, boys."

Luke was still standing there. Too close. "We *will* have that talk," he said so that only she heard him. "I promise you that."

A few minutes later, her children around her, eggs fried, breakfast to put on the table, Honor's foolishness receded and her confidence returned. "Luke, you're welcome to a breakfast sandwich, the same as the rest of us." She indicated the chair he had been sitting in before. "Greta, bring Anke's high chair here." She waved to the space beside her own seat, trusting her daughter's sloppy eating habits to keep Luke at a proper distance, letting him see the wall between them. She ushered her family to the table, shushing the children with a glance and bowing her head for silent grace.

Please God, she whispered inwardly. *Give me strength to deal with Luke, to move on with my life, to use him for what we need and then send him on his way, gracefully.* She opened her eyes to find Luke watching her, and she used the excuse of her children to look away. Her heart raced as her hands performed the familiar tasks of stacking eggs, scrapple and cheese on biscuits and pouring milk for her sons and daughter.

Luke went to the stove for another cup of coffee. "Some for you?" he asked.

She hated to ask any favors of him, but she did want the coffee. She needed more than one cup to get through the morning. Reluctantly, she nodded. *"Danke."*

He carried it to the table, added cream and placed the mug carefully in front of her plate. The children and Greta chattered. Anke giggled and cooed and tossed pieces of biscuit and egg onto the floor where the dog and cat vied for the best crumbs.

"I thought I'd start here in the kitchen, if that suits

you," Luke said after finishing off his second egg-and-scrapple sandwich.

"It would suit me best if you weren't here at all," she reminded him and then realized how ungrateful she sounded. She needed the work done. The state of the kitchen was hardly fit for her children—for anyone to prepare food or eat in. "I'm sorry," she said. "That was unkind. *Ya*, it would be good if you started in here. It certainly needs it."

So much of what Silas had promised had been left undone. And not for lack of funds, a truth she hadn't realized until after he had passed and she had taken the family finances into her hands. They were by no means poor, as he'd always led her to believe. Whatever his reasons for making her think that, he'd taken them with him to Heaven. And it would do no good to think ill of him. "Excuse me, Anke needs tidying up. Greta, see to the children."

She lifted a squirming Anke out of her high chair and carried her out of the kitchen and upstairs to the bathroom. There, she placed the toddler on a clean towel and proceeded to wash her face and hands, and wipe most of the egg and biscuit from her infant's gown. "It's going to be a new start for us, isn't it, baby?" she said to the child. "We'll make our house all sound and tidy and the matchmaker will find you a new *daddi*. Won't you like that?"

Anke needed a father, and the boys certainly needed one. That was what she had told Sara when she'd sat down in her office over a month ago to discuss an appropriate match. They needed a father with a steady but kind hand. Honor spoiled her children. Everyone said so. And she knew she did, but that was because Silas hadn't…

She bit off that line of thought. She wouldn't allow herself to wallow in self-pity. She had her faith, her children and her future to think of. She summoned a smile for Anke, tickled her soft belly and thrilled to the sound of baby laughter. She'd dealt with problems before, surely some greater than having Luke Weaver in her house. She'd find a way to manage him.

"After all," she said to her daughter, "how long can he be here? A few days? A few weeks? And then…" She lifted Anke in the air and nuzzled her midsection so that the baby giggled again. "And then we're done with him."

Freeman Kemp swung the bag of chicken feed into the back of Sara's wagon. "It's good of you to take this to Honor. Saves her a trip. And I'm glad you're going to do repairs on the house. That farm was in bad shape when Silas bought it, and I don't think he made many improvements before he took sick."

"It has to be difficult for a young widow with the children, just trying to get to the daily chores," Luke replied. "I can't imagine trying to get to bigger projects." He'd liked Freeman the moment he met him. Met him again. They had known each other as teenagers. Not well, but they'd once played on the same softball team.

"Our church community is getting so big that it's time we split off," Freeman said. "And it's natural that those of us farther out should form the new church. We're all hoping Honor will find a husband willing to settle here. You know how it goes. One young Amish family settles in an area and others usually follow."

Freeman tugged the brim of his hat down to shade his eyes from the glare of the setting sun. "You know," he said slowly. "Honor's mourning time is over. And you're a single man. Maybe you ought to think about courting her. 'Course you'd need a new hat." He offered a half smile. "She'd make someone a good wife. Honor's a sensible woman. Smart. Capable. And she speaks her mind."

"That she does." Luke grinned. Some men didn't like a woman who didn't hold back with their opinions, but he didn't have a problem with it. In fact, he wanted a wife who could be his partner. And it was a partner's duty sometimes to present the opposite side of an argument. "Honor and I knew each other from childhood."

Freeman shrugged. "Sometimes that's best. No secrets between you, then." He hesitated, as if sizing Luke up. Then he went on. "I'll be honest with you. I didn't care all that much for Silas. He was moody. Always seemed an odd match to me, him being older and on the serious side. But who am I to say? My family had given me up for a lifelong bachelor until my wife, Katie, came along and set me straight. Why don't you join us for church next month when we have service here at our place? We always appreciate a new face."

"I'd like that," Luke said. "I've promised Sara I'll attend Seven Poplars so long as I'm staying with her, though."

"That's no problem, then," Freeman answered. "We hold ours on a different schedule." He thought for a moment. "Long trip every day. And I see you have Sara's rig." He pointed to the wagon. "If you think you'd like to be closer, we've got a spare room you're welcome to.

I'd have to check with my wife, but I'm sure it would be okay with her."

Luke met Freeman's gaze. "I might just take you up on that. Once…I get an idea of how long I'm going to be working for Honor." *Once I get an idea if she's going to kick me off her property*, he thought.

"Well, we can talk about it. I'm sure I'll see you at Sara's Epiphany party Saturday. Nobody wants to miss that." He offered Luke his hand. "Glad you're back. It's good to meet you again."

"And you," Luke said.

"Just a word to the wise," Freeman said as he opened the gate that led onto the hardtop road.

"Ya?"

"Honor's children can be a handful." He pointed at him. "Don't turn your back on them."

"Oh, I've already seen evidence of it. But boys can be mischievous. And those three are still little."

Freeman laughed. "Don't say I didn't warn you."

Chapter Four

Honor glanced out the window to where her three red-cheeked boys were playing in the snow. Justice had climbed up on the gate, and Tanner was pushing it open and shut while Elijah threw snowballs at them both.

At least, she guessed he was attempting to throw snowballs. His aim was good, but he hadn't quite mastered the art of forming fresh snow into a ball. It was probably for the best, she thought, because no one was crying yet. Even Greta, who was in the barnyard, tossing shelled corn to the chickens and ducks, seemed to be having a good time.

Honor was glad. It wasn't often that she saw Greta enjoying herself. The girl had been so homesick when she first arrived that Honor had seriously considered sending her home. However, Silas's sister had made it clear that she had a lot of mouths to feed and the wages Honor paid Greta were a blessing to the family. There were nine children still at home, and the father was disabled, his only income coming from what he earned fixing clocks. And as inexperienced as Greta seemed to be with most chores, she was better than no help at all for Honor.

"Have you got time to help me for a couple of minutes?" Luke asked, interrupting Honor's thoughts. "This would go faster if you could hold that end of the board."

She glanced at him standing at a window, a freshly cut board in his hand. She tried not to smile. She still didn't want him here, but she was astonished at the amount of work he'd gotten done in only three days. And it was amazing how easily he seemed to be easing into the household. The children were already trailing after him as if they had known him their whole lives. That rankled most of all. "Of course," she said as she put Anke in her play yard.

Honor wondered why she hadn't found someone to do this carpentry work sooner. But she knew why. It was her own fear of spending all her savings, leaving nothing to live on, as Silas had warned she would. Silas had made all the financial decisions in their marriage. He'd even given her an allowance for groceries and household items. And now that she was free to make her own decisions, it had taken some time begin to trust her own judgment.

"Just hold this end," Luke instructed, indicating a length of wood. "The kitchen will feel a lot snugger once these leaks around the window are patched. Just some decent framing and some caulk is all you needed here."

It already felt a lot warmer. The first thing that Luke did every morning when he arrived was to chop wood and fill the wood box. She could cut wood, and she was capable of carrying it. But it was hard work. Luke made it seem easy. Of course, she had propane heat to fall back on, but firewood from her own property was free.

Honor grabbed her end of the board and held it in place.

"Something smells wonderful," he said between the strikes of his hammer. The nails went in true and straight. "Downright delicious," he persisted.

She sighed. "I'm making a rice pudding. I put it in the oven while you were rehanging the gate."

He glanced out the window to where all three of the children were now swinging on the gate. "It looks like those hinges are getting a thorough quality-control inspection."

Honor laughed. "That's a nice way of putting it. Most people aren't quite so charitable."

"They ought to be. They're fine youngsters."

"Danke." She thought so, even if they were full of mischief. But that was natural, wasn't it? Boys were mischief makers. It was their nature.

Luke pushed another piece of trim into her hands. "Line the bottom of that up with the horizontal board."

"Like this?"

"Just a little higher. There. That's perfect." He quickly drove several finishing nails into place. "A little paint and this window will give you another ten years of service."

"I can do the painting," she offered. "At least in here." She wanted the trim and ceiling white. The walls were a pale green, lighter than celery. She liked green, and the white trim would set it off and make the room look fresh.

"You're welcome to it, if you can find the time. Painting isn't one of my favorite tasks. I can do it if I have to, but I'm happier with the woodworking." He motioned to the corner of the room where he'd pulled up a section of cracked and worn linoleum. "The original floor is under here. White pine, I think. Wide boards. If we took up all the linoleum and refinished the floor, it would be a lot cheaper than putting down another floor covering." He met her gaze. "What do you think?"

She considered. "A saving when there was so much money to go out would be a blessing, but…" She frowned, trying to think how to word her thought delicately, then just said what was on her mind. "You think the children will ruin it?"

"I suppose it's possible," he said with a twinkle in his eyes. "But more than one family of children has lived in this kitchen over the last two hundred years, so I doubt it. The hardwood would come up beautiful."

"And plain?"

"As plain as pine." He chuckled and she found herself smiling with him. "Plain enough to suit a bishop."

"And we want to do that, don't we?" she replied.

Staying within the community rules was a necessary part of Amish life, one that she'd never felt restricted her. Rather, it made her feel safe. The elders of the church, the preachers and the bishop, told the congregation what God expected of them. All she had to do was follow their teaching, and someday, when she passed out of this earthly existence, she would be welcomed into Heaven. It was a comforting certainty, one that she had dedicated her life to living.

Anke pulled herself to her feet and tossed a rag doll out of her play yard onto the floor. Luke scooped it up and handed it back to her. She promptly threw it a second time, giggling when he retrieved it yet again.

"It's a game," Honor said. "She'd keep it up all day if you'd let her." She wiped her hands on her apron. "Look at the time. I'd best get the dumplings rolled for dinner."

Luke handed the doll to Anke again, then tickled her belly through the mesh side of the play yard. The baby giggled. "She was born after her father passed, wasn't she?" he mused.

Honor nodded. "She was."

"It must have been terribly difficult for you, not having him with you. And after, when Anke was an infant."

Honor thought carefully before she responded. She wasn't going to lie to make her late husband out to be someone he wasn't, but she wouldn't disrespect him, either. "Silas was a good man, but he believed that small children were the responsibility of the mother. He said he would take them in hand when they were older."

How old, she wasn't certain. Tanner hadn't been old enough to command his father's attention beyond Silas's insistence that their little boy hold his tongue at the table, in church and whenever adults were present. As for Justice and Elijah, she couldn't recall Silas ever holding one of them in his arms or taking them on his lap. Not to read to them. Certainly not to snuggle with them. Looking back, she could see that her decision to marry Silas had been impulsive, she'd agreed without really thinking through her options. If she was honest with herself, the truth was, she married Silas because he was the first man to ask. After Luke.

"I'm so sorry that you had to—"

"Don't be sorry for me, Luke," she interrupted, shaking her head. "We all have trials to live through. They say that God never gives anyone more than they can bear."

His green eyes filled with compassion. "I'm still sorry."

"Silas left me a home and four healthy children. Riches beyond counting," she murmured, turning away from him to take a dish towel from the back of one of the kitchen chairs. "I'm truly blessed."

Luke was quiet for a moment and then said, "So what do you think?"

"About what?" She turned back to him.

"The floor? Will you be satisfied with the old wood planks?"

"How will you finish them?"

"A high-grade poly. But it still won't cost much."

She held up her hand. "Say no more. We can try it. If I don't like it, I can always cover the floor again." She lifted a heavy cast-iron kettle from the countertop.

"Let me get that." Luke took it from her and carried it to the stove. "What's going with those slippery dumplings?"

"Fried chicken, peas, mashed potatoes and biscuits," she said, fighting a smile as she washed her hands at the sink. The man did like to eat.

"Mmm, sounds good. You don't suppose you could spare a bowl of dumplings."

"Didn't Sara pack you a lunch?"

He grinned. "She did. But it's a ham sandwich and an apple. Cold. Hot chicken and slippery dumplings sounds much tastier. Especially on a chilly day like this."

He was right. It did. Her stomach rumbled at the thought of hot biscuits dripping with butter and chicken fried crispy brown. She loved to eat, too, and she had no doubt that by the time she reached middle age, she'd have lost her girlish figure. Not that she looked much like the slim, wide-eyed girl who'd married Silas King. Four children coming so quickly had added inches to her waist and hips. It was only long hours and hard work that kept her from becoming round.

"So, am I to fast on Sara's charity, or are you willing to give me just the tiniest cup of dumplings?" Luke began plaintively.

He sounded so much like a little boy that Honor had to chuckle. "All right, all right, you can have dinner with us. But you'd best not waste Sara's ham sandwich." Honor began to remove flour and salt from the Hoosier cabinet she'd brought with her to the marriage. The piece had been her great-grandmother's, and it had been carefully cared for over four generations. The paint was a little faded, but she loved it just the way it was.

"I'll eat it on the way back to her house," Luke promised. He tucked several nails into his mouth and finished up the last piece of trim work on the window frame. "I replaced the sash cord so the window will go up and down easier," he said. "And you won't have to prop it open with a stick anymore."

"Danke," she said. Now, if he could just do something with the ceiling. It was low, which made the room darker than she liked. And crumbles of plaster sometimes fell on them. Once, she'd had to throw away a whole pot of chicken soup when a big chunk dropped into their supper.

The kitchen was one of the worst rooms in the house. Silas had promised that he'd get to it, but he never had. The parlor, he'd remodeled. Partially. Silas had said that he was making it a proper place for the bishop to preach, but he'd never asked the bishop to come. Instead, the room had become Silas's retreat from the children and from her. He would close the door and huddle in there with a blanket around his shoulders against the chill while he went over his financial records.

"What do you think?" Luke asked her.

Honor blinked. She wasn't sure what he'd asked her but didn't want to admit that she'd been woolgathering. "I'm not sure," she ventured as she measured out three level cups of flour.

"It would save time. And I'd get more work done here because I could work until dark."

She turned to him, realizing she had no idea what he was talking about. "I'm sorry?"

"If I stayed at the mill instead of driving back and forth to Sara Yoder's every day. Freeman invited me. He said I was welcome to stay in the farmhouse, but I didn't want to be a burden on Katie. And they're not married that long, so I think they should have their privacy. But…there's a little house for a hired man. Just a single room. The boy who works for him still lives with his parents a mile away, so the place is empty. I offered to rent it from them, but Freeman wouldn't have it. He says if I help them out a few hours on Saturday morning, when they have the most customers, I can live there for free."

"It sounds a sensible arrangement, but you won't be working on my house for long. What would you do then? Wouldn't you be better situated closer to Dover?"

"The mill will be fine. I don't know how long it will take to finish your house, but honestly…" He scratched his head. "There's a lot that needs fixing around here, Honor. Some things, like that windmill, have to be rebuilt. I can't go on using Sara's mule. It's not fair to her."

"What were you doing for transportation in Kansas?"

"I have horses. A neighbor is keeping them for me until I can find someone reliable to transport them to Delaware. Freeman says I can keep them at his place once they arrive." He shrugged. "Meanwhile, I can easily walk from the mill to your place."

"In bad weather?"

"Rain and snow don't bother me. After Kansas, Delaware weather will be mild."

"I'll remind you of that when you're soaking to the skin and wading through mud puddles." She shrugged. "Do as you please," she said, but secretly she thought it was a splendid idea. Who could complain about getting more work out of a hired man? And that's all Luke was, she told herself firmly. All he could ever be to her.

"You're certain you don't want to ride with us?" Freeman asked. "Plenty of room." He stood just inside the door of the little house he'd helped Luke to move into the night before.

The small log structure stood in the shadow of the mill within the sound of the millrace and shaded by willows in summer and spring. Wood-floored and low-ceilinged, the single room contained a bed, a braided rug on the floor, a table and two chairs, a propane stove and a built-in cupboard. It was sparse but spotless with a cheery red-and-white quilt and plain white curtains at the two narrow windows. Hand-carved pegs held his coat, water-damaged hat and spare shirt. It was a solid place for a man who needed a roof over his head close to a certain woman's house and one that Luke hoped he wouldn't have need of for long.

Luke shook his head. "*Ne*, you and your family go

on. I'll be fine. I want to shine my boots and shave. I'll catch a ride with Honor and the children."

Freeman nodded. "I can understand how you'd rather go with them." He grinned and glanced around the cabin. "I hope you'll be comfortable here. Anything you want, you know you're welcome to come up to the house. And we expect you to eat with us whenever the widow doesn't feed you."

He chuckled. "Sara Yoder thinks highly of you. And it's not always easy to make an impression on our matchmaker. Well—" he slapped the doorjamb "—see you there. Sara's Epiphany suppers are talked about all year. Every woman that comes brings her special dish, and we make up for the morning's fasting by stuffing ourselves like Thanksgiving turkeys."

"I can't wait." Luke remembered Honor saying something about the sweet potato pies she was planning on making the previous night, after he left and the children went to bed. "And thanks again for your hospitality," he said to Freeman.

The miller tugged on his hat and went out, and Luke hunted up the shoe polish and cleaning cloth he'd seen on the shelf in the miniscule bathroom. He'd lost all his good clothes in the bus accident and hadn't had the time to replace them. Until he bought a new wardrobe, he'd have to make do with the borrowed shirts and trousers that didn't quite fit. Not that he wasn't grateful to Sara and Hiram and Freeman for their kindness, but it was hard for him to be on the receiving end of charity when he'd been accustomed to being the one giving a helping hand to those who needed it.

Luke waited until he heard Freeman's buggy roll out of the mill yard before donning his coat and hat.

He hoped he hadn't waited too long and missed Honor. But he was counting on the children to keep her from leaving early. He hadn't exactly made arrangements to ride with her, and it would be a long walk to Sara's if things didn't work out. Or if Honor said no. Which he wasn't even going to consider.

The wind was rising as he strode away from the cabin and past the mill. There would be no customers today. The "closed, come again" sign hung at the entrance to the drive. Across the way and down, at the dirt pull off, he saw a blue pickup parked, and beyond it, at the pond's edge, a man and a small boy. It was too cold for fishing but they stood close together, tossing pebbles into the water and laughing about something.

A father and his son, Luke thought. A pang of regret knifed through him. If he'd not made the decision he had, Honor's children might have been his own. He could have been the man standing with his son beside the millpond, laughing with him, lifting him high in the air. So many years lost...so many possibilities that could never be. He swallowed hard as a lump formed in his throat.

For an instant, he could picture Honor's beautiful face the day before he'd ruined everything. She'd been radiant, joy in her movement, her features. And he'd crushed her happiness, turning her shining day to one of tearful sorrow. God forgive him, the fault was his. But...

He sighed deeply. If he were given the chance to relive that day, would he do any different? He'd never know, because that wasn't a possibility. All he had was hope that he could make a new beginning here and now.

Luke walked out onto the main road and headed toward Seven Poplars, hoping to he hadn't missed her buggy. As he walked, he wondered why Silas King had ever picked a farm this far away from Dover.

The nearest Amish school was a distance away. Tanner hadn't started school yet, although he was old enough, but when he did, it would be quite the walk for a first grader. Unless Honor planned on driving him at least part of the way, though that would mean leaving the other children in Greta's care or hauling them all back and forth every day.

It didn't make a lot of sense, but the boy had to attend school eventually. The Amish here had won the right to keep their children in their own schools from kindergarten through the eighth grade. And every child had to attend, so Tanner would have to start soon or someone from the state would be paying a call on Honor.

He'd ask her what she planned to do. But he'd have to do so in a way that didn't seem to be critical of her parenting. Honor was touchy over her children. Not that she wasn't a good mother. It was clear to him that her world revolved around them. But he had to agree with the warnings he'd gotten about them so far—the children *were* a little wild. And he couldn't help noticing that the consequences she promised for bad behavior never seemed to materialize.

Luke stopped and looked behind him. Still no sign of Honor. The fear that she had already passed this spot nagged at him. Wouldn't he look foolish, turning down Freeman's offer of a ride and then having to walk all those miles?

He was truly starving. He'd had no breakfast today. Not even coffee. Nothing more than a pint of cold water from a Mason jar. Freeman was probably halfway to Sara's by now. Maybe even pulling into the yard. Luke could imagine filling his plate with ham, turkey, roast beef and all the sides. He'd save room for a slice or two of Honor's sweet potato pie.

The sound of something coming behind him made him stop his daydreaming and look over his shoulder. But it wasn't a horse and buggy, just a car. The driver waved and drove on past. Luke glanced at the sky. What time was it? Well past noon. Why hadn't he left Freeman's place sooner? All he could think about was spending the day with Honor, and now it seemed he'd—

His heart leaped at another sound. There was a buggy coming. Grinning, he turned back toward Sara's house and started walking, taking long strides. He hadn't missed her. Things were working out exactly as he planned. There was no way she could pass him by without stopping to give him a ride. Not on Epiphany.

He started whistling a tune. He could hear the sound of horse's hooves on the blacktop. He didn't look back, just kept walking until the horse pulled alongside him. Then he turned, feigned surprise and waved at Honor and the children.

The children shouted, "Luke! Luke! Happy Epiphany!"

He grinned. "Happy Epiphany!" And then his smile faded as Honor smiled and waved and kept driving. The buggy rolled past him and on, down the road with the laughing children peering out the back and waving, leaving him behind.

Chapter Five

Honor waved at Luke and smiled back. Then she drove right by him without reining in the horse one bit. The nerve of the man. He'd wheedled his way into her house, forced her to hire him to make the repairs and now was manipulating her, so that she'd have to bring him to Sara's Epiphany supper.

He'd probably planned this whole thing; he'd probably been waiting there on the road for her since dawn. But she wasn't going to give him a ride. Why should she? Arriving together would give everyone in the community the idea that they were seeing each other. And that was definitely, positively, absolutely not happening.

"Mommi!" Tanner yelled. "That was Luke. You have to stop for him."

"Luke! Luke!" Justice had the back window partially open and was waving frantically.

Anke began to fuss. And she'd almost been asleep in Greta's arms before the boys had started such a racket.

"You should stop for him," Greta said.

Honor turned to look at Greta and guilt settled over her shoulders. What was wrong with her? She wouldn't leave any Amish person walking when she could offer a ride, especially when she knew Luke was going to the same destination she was.

Before she realized what she was doing, she pulled back on the leathers. "Whoa, whoa."

The children in the back of the buggy cheered and Greta uttered a small sound that might have been astonishment. Honor leaned out. "Well, what are you waiting for?" she called. "Hurry up. Get in. We're late as it is."

"What shall I do?" Greta whispered to Honor. "Should I get in the back?" The cheering behind them had become a chant of Luke's name. All three boys were bouncing up and down and waving their arms.

"Quiet, all of you," Honor warned. "*Ne*, you will not get in the back, Greta. Just slide over toward me. There's plenty of room for him. You don't take up as much room as a small rabbit." Honor made her face stern and stared straight ahead at the horse.

Luke got up into the buggy, taking the place beside Greta on the bench seat. *"Danke,"* he said with a grin. "I thought you were going to leave me to walk to Sara's."

"I considered it," Honor admitted, not looking at him. She clicked to the horse. "Walk on," she commanded. She was gripping the reins tighter than she needed to. Her palms were damp where the leathers lay against them.

"I can drive, if you like," Luke said.

"And why would I let you do that?" she asked. Then she felt a little silly. She had no proof that he'd deliberately trapped her into driving him. Maybe he'd missed Freeman. Or maybe the miller's plans had changed.

Anke was still fussing, and now she was trying to climb out of Greta's arms into Honor's.

"Suit yourself," Luke said, still maintaining that good-natured air that made her wish she belonged to a less peaceful people, because a tiny, unpleasant part of her wanted to give him a sharp kick in the shins.

Anke's griping became a wail. Greta struggled to hold on to the baby.

"You're right," Honor said, giving up and passing Luke the reins. "You should be driving." She held out her arms for her daughter and Greta gratefully passed her over. Honor reached into her coat pocket and found a pacifier. She popped it into the baby's mouth, and soon the tempest passed.

Greta shrank down so that she left a space between herself and Luke. She sniffed and wiped at her nose. Honor found a handkerchief in her other coat pocket and passed it to the girl. Luke drove in silence, his hands gentle on the reins. In the back, the boys grew silent.

Honor wondered at her own show of bad temper. How could she have done such a spiteful thing? What kind of example was that for a mother? "I'm sorry," she said softly to Luke. "I thought you'd deliberately waited for me on the road and…"

"You always did jump to conclusions," Luke said. "You should wait and find out, before you fly off the handle. Simon Beechy lives a ways down on this road. I met Simon at the mill the other day and he told me I was welcome to ride with him to Sara's." Luke looked at her with an amused expression. "Maybe I was taking him up on that offer."

She hesitated, looking him in the eyes. "And were you?" she asked. "Because it will be no trouble to let you out at Simon's."

"Ne, danke," he answered solemnly, looking straight

ahead again. "I think I'd rather ride with you and the children."

Anke gurgled and began to clap her hands together. Greta didn't make a sound. Honor glanced at her to make sure she was still breathing. The girl was very pale, but her round eyes were large in her face. She seemed scared to death to be sitting so close to Luke. Honor felt sorry for her. Greta really would need to toughen up.

Everyone was quiet again. The sound of the buggy wheels and the rapid clip-clop of the horse's hooves against the hardtop were all Honor could hear. She waited for Luke to say something. If this was a game of wits, she wanted to win. But he shouldn't give up so easily.

"So, which was it?" Honor pressed when she could hold her tongue no longer. "You wanted to get to Simon's, or it was a trick to get me to feel sorry for you?" This time she didn't look at Luke, but kept her gaze on Anke.

Tanner giggled, and Justice and Elijah took up the laughter.

"Hush, boys," Luke admonished softly.

To Honor's astonishment, they obeyed.

"I guess we'll never know the answer to that," Luke said, looking her way.

And, in spite of herself, Honor chuckled. One thing you could say for Luke. He might be infuriating, but he was never dull.

When they arrived at Sara's, her hired man, Hiram, and another man were taking charge of the guests' horses. Luke helped Greta out of the buggy and then came around to assist Honor. The boys scrambled out of the back, and Luke insisted on carrying the baskets with the sweet potato pies inside.

Sara's house was crowded with people, all talking at once in a mixture of *Deitsch* and English. Children, hers and others', crawled under the tables and hid behind the couch and easy chairs, peeked shyly at each other and then slipped away to play. Seniors sat or stood in clusters and younger women hugged and called out to friends.

The rooms smelled deliciously of gingerbread, pumpkin pie and baking ham, and everyone was relaxed and eager to share the day with each other. Although Seven Poplars wasn't the community that Honor had been raised in, she knew many of Sara's friends and immediately felt at home.

Hannah, Sara's cousin, who lived nearby, asked to take the baby, and Anke seemed delighted to be snatched away and displayed for everyone to admire. The schoolteacher, Ellie, who was a little person, showed Honor where to put her coat and introduced her to several young women Honor hadn't yet met. Luke deposited the pies on a counter on the porch with other desserts and vanished, presumably to find other men. In social occasions, Amish men and women were free to circulate as they pleased, but usually they ended up talking with those of their own gender. For Honor, having other women to talk to was wonderful, given her isolation on the farm.

Sara greeted her with a kiss on the cheek and a request for help with biscuit dough that was almost ready to go into the oven. Honor readily accepted the task, found an apron to cover her good clothes and joined Ellie in hand rolling baking powder biscuits and putting them on trays to go into the oven. Rebecca, one of the Yoder sisters, joined them in the kitchen.

Rebecca was wife to a Seven Poplars preacher and they had three children. Honor had met her before, but they'd never really had a chance to talk. With her in the kitchen now, Honor soon learned that Rebecca had a delightful sense of humor.

It was such a treat to be there, enjoying Sara's hospitality. Before her marriage to Silas, Honor had always enjoyed visiting friends and relatives and sharing the joy of holidays such as Little Christmas. Silas hadn't. He preferred to remain at home, and he preferred her in the house with her duties and her children. Church and the occasional grocery-shopping trip had been the rare times when she'd gotten out. Why she'd waited so long after his passing to return to the community, she wasn't sure. But she was here, and she was determined to make the most of every moment.

Men were setting up extra tables in the living room and the sitting room at the bottom of the stairs. Honor noticed a woman in a black elder's *kapp* and knit shawl sitting in the midst of several young mothers. The old woman, who was in a wheelchair, fussed loudly as one of them arranged a blanket over her knees and passed a baby into her arms.

"That's Anna Mast's grandmother Lovina Yoder," Ellie explained. "She lives with Anna and her Samuel."

"I remember her. She's Martha Coblenz's mother, isn't she?" Honor asked.

"Ya," Ellie agreed. "And Hannah's mother-in-law. Not Albert's mother, but her first husband's."

Honor lowered her voice. "Lovina's always terrified me."

Ellie chuckled. "*Ya*, she can be that way. But Hannah says Anna gets along *goot* with her."

Sara took Lovina a cup of hot mulled cider and retrieved the baby. Lovina complained that the cider wasn't hot enough and demanded to know when supper was to be served.

"Soon, soon," Sara soothed, patting the elderly woman's hand. "We're just waiting on the biscuits and a few more families."

"I should hope so," Lovina declared. "I didn't come out on such a cold day to go home with an empty stomach. My Jonas is hungry, too. He told me so. He's out in the barn. Milking the cows. But he will be in soon, and he wants his supper."

Honor looked at Ellie and whispered, "I thought Jonas passed away long ago."

"He did," Ellie said. "But Lovina likes to think he's still with us. Her memory isn't what it used to be, so Anna thinks it's kinder if we all just go along with it."

A woman brought a new, partially knit baby cap for Lovina to admire, and the elderly woman stopped grumbling and turned all her attention to the pattern.

Another couple came in out of the cold, bringing plates of German sausages, a tub of sauerkraut and a huge platter of *fastnacht kucha*. Since honey doughnuts were Honor's weakness, she couldn't wait for dessert.

Honor wasn't certain how any more guests would fit into Sara's house, but no one seemed to mind that the rooms were quickly filling up or that yet another table had to be squeezed in.

Between the exchange of recipes and neighborhood news, Honor couldn't help hearing snatches of Luke's voice or catching glimpses of him. To her own astonishment, she found herself following him with her gaze. Was it possible that she still cared for him after what had happened between them? She knew the answer to that question, but it had nothing to do with her resolve that he could have no part in her future other than to mend a few broken fences or patch a hole in a wall.

"I see you came with Luke Weaver," Rebecca teased as they completed the final tray of biscuits and slid it into the hot oven.

"What?" Honor felt herself flush. Had it been so obvious that she was watching him? "Um, we came upon him walking. On the road."

Ellie chuckled. "And, naturally, you gave him a ride."

Honor offered a quick smile. "Naturally." She spotted Anke in Martha Coblenz's arms and took the opportunity to escape the conversation by swooping to reclaim her daughter. "*Aenti* Martha. It's good to see you." Honor raised on tiptoe to kissed the older woman's cheek. "How is *Onkel* Reuben?" Martha wasn't really a relative, but she'd been a good friend of Honor's late mother, and Honor had always addressed them as Aunt and Uncle.

"Not well," Martha replied. "Not well, at all. His back and his knees. He suffers in cold weather."

Honor smiled and nodded as though she hadn't seen *Onkel* Reuben carrying one end of a heavy table just a few minutes before. Like his wife, Reuben was full of complaints. As Honor's mother had always said, Reuben had never been one for work, but he'd always eaten for two men and seemed to do whatever he wanted. But despite their dour outlooks on life, Honor had always believed the couple had good hearts.

"Sara's hunting you a husband, is she?" Martha asked. "About time." She was a tall, spare woman with an ample chin and a nose like a hawk's, who never missed an item of interest that went on in the county.

Honor nodded. "I've asked Sara to find me a settled, older man, possibly a widower with children. I need someone with experience to be a father to my children."

Martha harrumphed, "That you do, because they are sore in need of a man's hand, I can tell you that. Remember what the Good Book says—spare the rod and spoil the child."

"Martha!" Hannah Yoder Hartman entered the kitchen, bundled in cape and bonnet, her nose and cheeks red from the cold winter air. She was carrying a cast-aluminum turkey roaster. "Could you get this lid? I think it's slipping."

Martha grabbed a hot mitt off the counter and successfully caught the sliding cover. Hannah deposited the turkey onto Sara's second stove.

"Come with me," Martha urged her sister-in-law. "It's warm in here, and I have something to tell you. You'll never guess..."

Hannah followed Martha out of the kitchen, and Honor gave a sigh of relief. She feared that bringing Luke in her buggy might start gossip, but she hoped that she'd stopped that rumor before it got started.

Greta appeared at Honor's side. "Can I take Anke?" she asked. "I was telling some girls my age about her, and they wanted to see her."

Surprised that Greta would ask for her daughter, Honor happily handed her over as she made the introductions to the others in the kitchen. "Greta is Silas's niece, come to help me with the children," she explained. "She doesn't know many people here in Seven Poplars yet."

"But I met Jane now," Greta said. "And her sister May. They have a little sister the same age as Anke. And there's a girl, Zipporah, who lives near us, I think. They asked if I could bring her." She pointed to the front room. "There are blocks. For Anke to play with."

"Of course," Honor agreed. "I'm glad you're making new friends." She watched until Greta was safely out of earshot and then smiled at Rebecca. "That's a blessing. The girl's been so homesick that I was afraid I'd have to send her back to her mother. She didn't want to come today. I do hope she has a good time."

"She will," Rebecca said.

"Ya," Ellie chimed in. "Jane and May are my students. They're nice girls. And they are experienced with babies, so your Anke's in safe hands."

Rebecca turned to the sink and began to wash the large stainless steel bowl that had held the biscuit dough. "I was surprised to hear that Luke Weaver's come back from Kansas. Is he planning on staying in Delaware?"

Honor shrugged. "I wouldn't know. He's doing some carpentry work for me."

"Mmm-hmm," Rebecca answered. She and Ellie exchanged glances and both women chuckled.

"Ne, really," Honor protested. She suddenly felt her throat and cheeks growing warm again and told herself that it was the heat of the oven. "It's just a business arrangement."

Ellie's voice dropped to a whisper. "But you have to admit, he *is* cute."

Honor shrugged. "I suppose, in a boyish sort of way."

Ellie giggled. "Not boyish by the width of those shoulders."

Sara walked back into the kitchen with a pitcher in

her hands. "Honor, would you go down to the cellar for more apple cider? That door over there. Watch the steps. There isn't much light from the basement window today."

Ellie looked up from unwrapping squares of homemade butter pressed with a leaf print. "I can go, if you like."

"*Ne*, I don't mind." Honor took the green pitcher and slid the latch on the cellar door. She waited a few seconds at the top of the steps while her eyes adjusted to the dim lighting. When they'd arrived at Sara's, the sun had been shining, but now the afternoon was growing cloudy and there wasn't much light coming in through the windows.

Honor descended the stairs and quickly found the keg of cider. She filled the pitcher and started for the steps, but, as she put her hand on the banister, someone opened the door. She stepped back and saw that it was Luke. He was carrying a green pitcher.

"I didn't know you were down here," he said.

"I was just bringing up this pitcher of apple cider. For Sara."

For an instant, a puzzled expression crossed his face, but then he smiled. "Funny," he said. "Sara must have forgotten." He tilted his pitcher so that she could see that it was empty. "Because she just sent *me* for cider."

He chuckled, and then, against her will, she began to laugh with him. "If I didn't know better," she said, "I'd think Sara is trying to set us up."

Chapter Six

Leaving the door open, Luke came down the stairs and settled on one of the lower steps. He cradled the empty pitcher between his hands. "I suppose it's *possible* that Sara is trying to match us up. It is what she does for a living. And, from what I hear…" He met Honor's suspicious gaze full on. "She knows what she's doing. She has a reputation for seeing solid matches where others don't."

Honor pursed her lips, but her eyes were open wide, not narrowed, and she didn't appear to be disapproving.

Luke took it as a positive sign and forged ahead. "I already know we'd be a good fit. Perfect, in fact, if it wasn't for what happened last time you agreed to marry me. Which you have every reason to be angry about."

"I'm not angry. At least not anymore," she corrected, standing in front of him, holding a pitcher identical to the one Sara had given him. "That was a long time ago, and I've moved on with my life."

"I still feel like we need to talk about what happened," he urged, coming to his feet. "If you'd let me apologize for—"

"Ne," she interrupted firmly. "I'm afraid I'm not *that* far past it. Not today, at least." She sighed. "I don't want to feel those emotions again, Luke. Anger. Bitterness. That's not helpful for either of us. I'm simply not in the mood to drag all that up. This is too special of a day to ruin it with an old disagreement."

"We have to talk about it someday," he insisted.

"Maybe, maybe not." She shrugged. "But definitely not today. I'm having a wonderful time, and I don't want anything to ruin it."

He crossed the cellar to the barrel and filled his pitcher with cider. "This is delicious, you know," he said. "I had a glass upstairs. Some of the best I've had in years. Sara said she liked to blend different kinds of apples to get just the right flavor."

"Ya." Some of the tension eased from Honor's posture. She gave him a shy smile. "I had some, too, and it was good."

"Tanner definitely likes it. I think I saw him drink three cups." Luke grimaced. "I hope that won't cause trouble later."

"I don't think so," Honor replied, setting her pitcher on a stool. "He has a stomach like his father. Silas could eat anything and it never bothered him. Once, at his brother-in-law's house, the two of them were eating scrapple sandwiches and they hadn't bothered to cook the scrapple." She shook her head. "I like scrapple, but I want mine crispy and cooked all the way through. I was certain Silas would be sick, but it never even gave him indigestion. He said I was too finicky. That I'd make our boys weak."

"They hardly look weak to me." Luke tightened the shutoff on the cider barrel. "Justice can already lift Tanner, and in another year, Tanner won't be able to hold his own when they wrestle. And that little one, Elijah, he's amazing for his age. Anything the older two do, he's right there, trying to imitate them." He carried the pitcher back to the bottom of the steps and placed it carefully on the floor before sitting down again. He patted the step beside him. "Sit with me? I won't bite. Unless you think you'd better go up and check on the children."

Honor folded her arms and regarded him for a long moment. Then she lowered herself on the step beside him. "*Ne*, I don't want to check on the children. I don't hear any screams, and I don't hear anything breaking. There are enough pairs of eyes to watch them, and truthfully, I'm enjoying having someone else do it." She glanced away and he noticed a slight rosy tint on her cheeks. "Now I've said it," she murmured. "You'll think me a terrible mother."

"I don't. I think you're a wonderful mother…if a little—" He bit off what he was going to say, knowing that he was wading into uncertain depths.

"You think I spoil them?"

"Not spoil, exactly. But they are…" He let his last thought go unspoken.

"Bad? Wild? Unruly?" She laughed. "Go ahead, say it. You won't hurt my feelings. And you won't be the first to say it. I know that I sometimes let them go too far, but I don't believe a parent should always be telling a child not to do something. Don't you think it's better to be an example of how they should live than to be constantly dictating to them?"

"You're right, of course," he said. "And I don't think they're bad children. Wild, certainly. But not bad and not mean. They have your good nature. And they don't whine. I hardly ever hear them cry, not even the baby."

She arched a brow. "And you've had a lot of experience parenting small children?"

"*Ne*, of course not." It was his turn to shrug. "But I had a lot of cousins out in Kansas, and most of them are older than me. We had our fair share of children in our church community. Our preacher gave a lot of sermons on the responsibilities of being a mother or father and on the importance of bringing up children who would honor their parents and our traditions."

"Honoring your parents and doing what you're told was always important to Silas," Honor said. "But my mother and father always put love first. It's what I've tried to do with my little ones. It's not always easy, especially now, being both father and mother." She steepled her hands. "You'd be surprised at how much advice I get, especially from those who have no children of their own."

"Ouch," he said, grimacing. "Point taken." He chuckled and she laughed with him. "But I do think you're a wonderful mother," he said. "An amazing person who never deserved what I did to you."

Her eyes narrowed. "Didn't we agree we weren't going to discuss this?"

"Not really. You said we weren't. I never agreed." Half-surprised she didn't just stand and go upstairs, he pushed on. "I don't want to put a damper on your holiday, Honor. I'll make this quick, I promise, but I need to say it to you. Face-to-face." He took a breath and turned to her. "I made a terrible mistake the day we were supposed to marry, and it's troubled me all these years. I owe you an apology. I hurt you, and I'm sorry. I know it doesn't make up for what I did, but I hope you can find it in your heart to forgive me. If not now, someday."

She looked away.

"I also need to try to explain how it was. I'm not trying to make excuses for myself, but looking back, I think I was too young to get married. *We* were too young. I thought I was ready, but as the day of our marriage got closer, I began to have doubts."

"About me," she said quietly. "Whether I was the right one."

"*Ne*. Never." He took her hand. "It was always about me. At the time, I wasn't positive I could live the Amish life. If I had the faith. Honor, I didn't know if I had the strength to be the kind of husband you deserved." He squeezed her hand. "I never doubted my faith in God, but I wondered if we were clinging to old ways too long when the rest of the world had moved on. And when it came time to go to the wedding that morning, I just couldn't…" His voice cracked and his eyes teared up. "I couldn't do it."

She raised her head and looked at him. He was afraid of what he would see in her eyes; he hadn't dared to hope for the sympathy, the compassion he found there.

"We *were* young," she said. "Me, especially. I had no idea what being a wife really meant. Not until I married Silas and found out." She gave him her other hand, and they sat there for a few seconds, not speaking, just feeling the warmth and security of each others' hands. "Thinking, back, I wonder if we'd just—"

The door at the top of the cellar steps abruptly slammed shut, interrupting her. Then they heard the latch slide into place and the sound of a child's laughter.

Luke got to his feet. "What's going on?"

"Justice would be my guess," Honor said, sounding amused.

Luke reached the top of the steps and tried the door. "Locked." He banged on the door. "Hey!" he called. "Let us… Let me out!" He glanced down at Honor. "Sorry."

"Not your fault." She pressed her lips together. "Unless I miss my guess, my little troublemaker is at it again."

He chuckled. "When you think about it, it is pretty funny."

She flashed him a smile so full of life and hope that it nearly brought tears to his eyes, a smile he'd been praying for all these years.

"I suppose it is," she agreed. "At least, it will be if someone lets us out before we become the scandal of the county."

"Right." He turned back to the door and rapped sharply. Seconds later, he was rewarded by the click of the latch and Sara's face in the doorway.

"I asked you to bring up cider," Sara said smoothly. "Not to lock yourselves in." She peered down to see Honor picking up the pitchers of cider and bringing them up the stairs. "Hurry along. We're just sitting down to the tables, and you don't want to miss silent prayer."

Luke met Honor halfway and took both pitchers from her. As they passed from hand to hand, he met her gaze. There was a twinkling in her eyes that made him think he might have accomplished what he hoped to today. Now that she was ready to forgive him, he was ready to bring up the possibility of courting. But not today.

Today, he'd have to be content with the memory of the feel of her hand in his and her beautiful smile.

There was a last-minute flurry of activity before the sit-down meal: babies reunited with their mothers, pre-school children seated at small tables with teenage girls to assist them, older boys separated from their sisters and cousins, and the best seats found for the elders. Satisfied that her little ones were all cared for and didn't need her, Honor allowed Rebecca to usher her to a table of young women near the kitchen. Honor had offered to help with serving, but Sara refused her.

"All the food is on the tables," Sara had answered. "Plates have been fixed for the toddlers and *Grossmama* Yoder. The rest can help themselves. Now, you just sit, eat and enjoy."

Rebecca's husband, Caleb, called for grace, and everyone hushed their chattering and lowered their heads. He didn't deliver a prayer, but he said a few words of welcome on Sara's behalf, reminding the guests of the significance of Epiphany after everyone had kept the traditional moments of silence. "Sara is so pleased that you could all be here to share Old Christmas with her," the young preacher concluded. "Now, let's give credit to the cooks and this good food, and eat."

As plates of turkey, roast pork, beef, bread and vegetables were passed around, Honor couldn't help but notice that Luke was seated on the end of the younger men's table, facing her. Rebecca, seated beside her, kept up a lively discourse with her half sister, Grace, another sister Leah, and their cousin Addy. Honor knew Addy because she was Aunt Martha's daughter, and Addy and her husband owned a butcher shop in Dover. Addy was expecting another baby sometime soon, and Honor had seen Aunt Martha fussing over her.

"It's not like this is your first," Rebecca said to Addy. "You had no problems giving birth once before, and look at Honor here. She's had four and is none the worse for wear."

"*Ya*, I know, I know. It's not me who's worried," Addy replied. "It's my mother. I'm sure it's because I'm her only daughter. But then, Gideon is nearly as bad. The other day, he was fussing because I carried in a tray of scrapple. Honestly, I feel fine, and my midwife says everything looks perfectly normal."

Honor took a forkful of mashed potatoes, glanced up and met Luke's gaze. He smiled at her, and she averted her eyes, but not before she smiled back at him. Talking to him in the cellar had been nice. As much as she'd told him that she didn't want to discuss their breakup, it had made her feel better to hear him admit that it had been his fault.

She took a sip of cider and toyed with her coleslaw, turning her fork around and around and staring at her plate. In all fairness, she had been the one who pressed him for the wedding. She should have known that he wasn't as enthusiastic as she was about marrying, even after he'd agreed. He'd even suggested they wait another year while he worked and saved more money. But she had been young and immature and had insisted, because she'd been infatuated by the idea of being a wife. She'd wanted to be able to call herself Luke's wife, but looking back, she realized that she'd had no idea what the role really meant. She'd wanted to marry him, and she'd wanted to do it that fall, not the next. So she had to accept some of the fault.

"Honor?" Grace held a saltshaker in her hand. "Could you pass this to Violet, please?"

"*Atch*, of course." Honor realized that she'd been lost in her own thoughts. She made an effort to pay closer attention to her tablemates and resolved not to keep stealing peeks at Luke. What if someone noticed? They might get the wrong idea. Making her peace with what had happened between her and Luke was one thing. It certainly didn't mean that she was interested in him. She didn't want to invite curiosity. Bad enough that Sara might have some notion of matching the two of them. Sara, she could deal with. But she didn't want to encourage Luke to think that he had a chance with her, because he didn't. Absolutely not. It was impossible. End of subject.

But not the end of the repercussions of her time alone with him in the cellar.

When the meal was finished and being cleared away, Aunt Martha cornered Honor and insisted she step into Sara's office so that they could talk without being overheard.

"I really need to pack up the children," Honor protested. "Baby Anke—"

Martha cut her off. "Your Anke is fine. Greta has her. What's the girl for if not to take some of the load off you? I've told my son-in-law—my Dorcas needs a girl to help her."

Honor nodded. When Aunt Martha said Dorcas, she meant Addy. Apparently, when Addy had met her husband-to-be, he preferred her middle name, so she'd asked everyone to call her Addy instead of Dorcas. Most people had, other than her mother. But then, Aunt Martha rarely did what people asked her. She had her own mind that was pretty much set in concrete on how things should be done.

Aunt Martha latched onto Honor's arm and clung to her elbow with a death grip. For a woman in her sixties, she was surprisingly strong. Tall and gaunt, with a sharp nose, recessed eyes and bony chin, Martha may have looked frail, but she was far from it. "You just come in here," she insisted. "Sara won't mind. You need to hear this. It's my duty as your mother's friend to tell you what people are saying."

Honor glanced around the room, caught sight of Sara and grimaced in a silent plea for help. Sara chuckled and threw up her hands as if to say, "You're on your own." Seeing her last hope of escape fading, and not wanting to attract any more attention than necessary Honor allowed the older woman to tug her into the office.

Once inside, Martha twisted around and used one hip to shut the door before planting herself solidly in front of it. From inside her voluminous skirt pocket she produced a much-folded and wrinkled sheet of newspaper and waved it in the air. "You haven't seen this, have you? I know you haven't. You're much too smart to ignore something like this."

Honor reached for the paper, but Aunt Martha pulled it back. "Shocking, really," she pronounced. "Although, considering the source, I don't suppose any of us should be surprised. What Sara can be thinking of, I'm sure I don't know. I thought she had more sense of decorum. Of course, she's not really a Yoder, you know. Just a Yoder by marriage. Her family doesn't have a lot of *goot* German stock, not like the Yoders."

Honor thought she recognized the paper in Honor's

hand as being part of the *Delaware State News*. "There's an article about Sara?" she asked.

Martha's mouth drew into a small pucker before she launched into another harangue. "Sara? Why ever would you think it was Sara? I've no bone to pick with Sara—other than her dubious choices in young men to marry off to our girls." She huffed. "*Ne*, not Sara. Luke. Luke Weaver."

Honor's brows knit. "The article is about Luke?"

Martha rested a hand on her hip as one shoe tapped the hardwood floor impatiently. "Honestly, Honor. Are you paying attention at all? Naturally, he wanted to keep it a secret. We take the paper. My Reuben always reads the paper after breakfast. And I'd used it to line the bottom of my egg basket, just as I always do. But then my Dorcas came by to get some extra eggs. She wanted to make a pound cake for Gideon. Dorcas makes the loveliest cakes. Anyway, she used up the last of the eggs, and then she saw it." Triumphantly, Martha held out the page. "There he is. Mystery cowboy, my eye. That's Luke Weaver. Dorcas recognized him right off. See for yourself." She pushed the news sheet at Honor.

Honor took it, went to Sara's desk and spread the page out, taking care to smooth the wrinkles. "It says this man saved the other passengers and the driver when the bus went into the water. The paper calls him a hero."

"The photograph. That's the real sin. And him probably bragging about his deeds and trying to take credit." Martha scoffed. "Probably exaggerated. That's what the *Englisher* do in their news. Everything is made to be bigger and worse than it is. Don't you remember when those two ducks got run over on Route One? The paper that day read Doomsday for Local Wildlife!"

Honor reread the news story and then scrutinized the photo. There was no doubt in her mind. The picture was of Luke, but where the *Englishers* had gotten the idea that he was a cowboy, she had no clue. "Surely, saving all those people is a good thing," she ventured.

Martha looked unconvinced. "You should never have let him do that work on your house. Not after what he did. Not him being what he is."

"And what is he?" Honor asked. Everyone in Seven Poplars knew that Martha often had her own interpretation of events and sometimes facts. One was wise to take what she said with a grain of salt. Still, that *was* Luke's photo, so there was some truth to the event.

"A deceiver." Aunt Martha waggled her finger. "A man whose word can't be trusted. And a man who enjoys being made a fuss over."

"That doesn't sound like the Luke I know," Honor said.

"Make no graven image. That's what the Bible tells us," Martha continued, ignoring Honor's comment. "And that." She pointed at the news page. "*That* is a graven image."

Honor considered the photo. Luke looked wet; the brim of his hat was drooping. But even as bedraggled as he was, he still looked pretty fine. "Maybe he couldn't help it. Maybe the English just took his picture without asking. It happens. Remember the Beachy twins at Spence's Auction last summer?"

Aunt Martha's eyes when round. "You aren't considering courting one of the Beachy twins!"

Honor was suddenly at a loss for words. "I'm not courting... Luke and I aren't..." she began, and then added, "Luke's just doing carpentry work for me."

"I wouldn't let him set one foot on my farm, if I were

you," Martha warned. "After he shamed you by leaving you on the day of your wedding. Shamed your family. All that creamed celery that we spent days preparing. I can tell you, it was a long time before your mother could hold up her head at quilting bees."

"I didn't know about this," Honor said as she glanced down at the news story. "He didn't say anything."

"And would he? He's sneaky, that's what he is. Luke Weaver is a sneak. No proper match for you. Your mother would turn over in her grave, you courting him again."

"But I'm not courting Luke."

Martha folded her arms. "Thank Providence for that. No telling what further trouble and shame I've saved you."

Honor folded the paper and handed it back to Martha, but the older woman shook her head.

"*Ne*, best you keep it. Show it to him. See what he has to say for himself." She reached for the door handle. "And while you're at it, ask him about his brother."

"What about his brother?" She knew that Luke had at least one older half brother, but she'd never met him.

"A lot he keeps hidden, I'd say. And everyone knows about that brother. He left the Amish to go to Nashville. A singer." She nodded to emphasize her words. "With one of those country-and-western bands. Maybe he's the one who lured Luke into pretending to be a cowboy."

"That doesn't sound right," Honor protested weakly. "I'm sure there's some mix-up…a mistake."

"Oh, there's a mistake, all right," Martha said. "It was when Sara Yoder brought Luke Weaver to your house." She yanked open the door. "And now it's up to you to send him packing."

Chapter Seven

It was late when families finally set aside their game boards and loaded sleepy children and the elderly into buggies. Greta had found a new friend, Zipporah King, a cousin to Susanna Yoder's husband, who had recently moved to the area. Zipporah and Greta were the same age and shared many of the same interests. When Greta had begged to have Zipporah come home to spend the night, Honor was pleased. Freckle-faced and giggly, Zipporah seemed just the remedy for Greta's homesickness.

"I'm seeing you all safely home," Luke had said firmly. "This is no hour for women and children to be on the road and going into an empty house alone."

With so many chaperones, Honor felt it was only sensible to accept his offer. Despite her concern over the newspaper article and Aunt Martha's warnings against Luke, Honor hadn't been looking forward to entering the dark farmhouse. For safety's sake, she'd left a battery-powered lamp on, but there would be the gloomy barn to face when she put away the horse.

As often as Silas had made her grit her teeth and pray

for patience, she missed his solid presence and his protection. It might be a foolish fear for a woman grown with a flock of children, but she'd always been a little afraid of the dark.

As they turned out of Sara's long driveway and onto the road, it began to snow again. A thin, pale covering of snowflakes frosted the road and the dried grass on either side.

"This is nasty weather," Honor said. "I hate to think of you walking back to the mill in this. Maybe we should drop you off and then go the rest of the way on our own."

"Ne." Luke shook his head, closing his gloved hands more tightly on the reins. "I'll see you inside with heat and light before I leave."

Honor felt a small twinge of relief. She'd tried. If he had to walk two miles home, it was on him. "You could take the horse," she suggested. "And the buggy."

"I could," Luke agreed with a slight nod. "We'll see what it's like after we get you and the children settled. We had a lot of snow in Kansas. Far more than this. And tonight is hardly a blizzard. It's barely freezing."

It felt colder to Honor. It was good to snuggle down under the blanket and let Luke drive the horse. Anke was already fast asleep, and Honor could feel her daughter's warm breath on her cheek. For once she felt calm and all seemed right in the world. Honor rocked her baby and uttered a silent prayer for this precious child and the others murmuring in the back of the buggy. How she loved her children. Until she became a mother, she'd not really known what love was. She would do anything to protect them, make any sacrifice.

Ahead of them was Samuel Mast's buggy, and behind

them were some of the large Beachy family. More than a
dozen buggies rolled and bumped down Sara's driveway
and then separated to continue on home. There were no
cars in sight. It was close to midnight, far too late for
the children to be awake, but everyone had been having such a wonderful time at Sara's party that no one
had wanted to be the first to leave. Tomorrow, for those
who had church services in their districts, there would
be yawns and sleepy eyes, but good memories. After all,
Epiphany came but once a year.

"Let's sing, shall we?" Luke said. And then to her,
quietly, he said, "If we can keep the children awake
until we get them home, they should be easier for you
to get into bed."

Again, she wondered at Luke's ease with her children. He always seemed to know what was best to do
or say to them to gain cooperation or turn disruptive
behavior to good. Anke was still shy with him, but Elijah, Tanner and Justice seemed to have accepted him
as part of the family. She knew that might cause some
difficulty when he finished the work on the house and
barns and had to leave, but she had decided to be grateful for it while she had it.

Their own father had never had much patience with
them or with childish games, and he certainly had not
encouraged them to sing with him. Had Silas *ever* raised
his voice in song? In service, certainly, as was expected
of a church member. But had he ever sung for the fun
of it or to soothe tired children? She didn't think so.

"Oh, Susanna," Luke sang loudly in English, "Don't
you cry for me. I come from Alabama, with a banjo on
my knee…"

"What's a banjo?" Justice demanded.

"I think it's an English chicken," Tanner supplied in *Deitsch*.

Honor chuckled. "A banjo isn't a chicken. It's an *Englisher* thing that makes sound…music."

Luke picked up the word and supplied *chicken* for *banjo* through the remaining verses, much to the delight of Zipporah and Greta, who sang backup.

One by one, the other buggies turned off the road and their blue and red flashing lights grew dim in the falling snow. Then Honor and Luke and the children were alone in the night, the horse moving gaily along, everyone inside the buggy warm and happy, singing together. "Oh, Susanna" was followed by "She'll Be Coming Around the Mountain" and then "Silent Night" in *Deitsch*. As the miles passed, the singers in the back grew fewer, and finally, it was just her and Luke to finish off the last chorus of "Jesus Loves Me" to the sound of Greta's snoring.

For a few moments there was only the swish of the battery-operated wipers and the muffled clicking of the horse's hooves, and then Luke said, "I guess my plan didn't work."

"I guess not," Honor replied and then chuckled. "But it *was* fun." So much fun, in fact, she admitted, that she was sorry when Luke reined in the horse to turn into her lane.

"It was," he murmured.

The snow was a little deeper in the driveway, but the fence posts on either side made it easy for the horse to see where it was going. The animal, sensing the warm barn and perhaps a scoop of grain, picked up the pace.

Go slower, Honor thought to herself. *Don't be in such a hurry, Luke.*

She didn't want the evening to end, and she didn't want to deal with more serious subjects like the length of Luke's employment and the newspaper article that she needed to talk to him about. Better to just enjoy the moment than to consider the consequences of what she might be encouraging. She was tired of making decisions all the time, of being responsible, of being in charge.

Anke stirred and sighed in Honor's arms, bringing back her sense of duty. She couldn't allow herself to be swayed by foolish thoughts or emotions that swirled like the snowflakes on the night air. Instead, she turned her mind to what Aunt Martha had told her. And of the photograph in the newspaper. "Luke, is it true?" she asked, her voice a little harsher than she'd intended.

"Is what true?"

Honor forced her voice to a whisper. "Martha showed me a photograph. In the newspaper. It looked like you. They said that there was an accident. With a bus."

He reined in the horse and they came to halt on the far side of the gate. *"Ya,"* he answered, turning to her on the bench seat. "It's true."

"You did those things? You saved those people from the water?"

"I could hardly climb out myself and leave them. There was a woman with a baby. And others. The driver was unconscious. He could have drowned. I had to do what I had to do." Luke sighed. "But I didn't ask to have my picture taken. You know how they are with their cell phones. The English. They take pictures of everything."

"You didn't give them your name," she observed. "If you had wanted to show off, I would think you would have told the newspaper people who you were."

"And I wouldn't have said I was a cowboy." She could feel him looking at her, even though she couldn't really see his eyes. "Believe me, Honor. All it did was make me feel foolish."

She narrowed her gaze. "So why did they call you a cowboy?"

He shrugged. "My church hat, I suppose. Someone not used to Amish clothing?"

She smiled in the darkness. The English could sometimes have some pretty funny ideas about the Amish. "Why didn't you say anything to me about saving those people?"

"How would I have brought up the subject? You would have thought I was bragging."

She thought about that for a moment. Maybe that first day she would have thought so. But not now. Now she knew him again. Better. "I think it was brave of you to help those people," she said softly. "You could have gotten out of that bus and left the *Englishers* to save themselves."

"Ne," he said simply. "I couldn't."

"Now I feel ashamed." She rested her chin on Anke's little head. "To question you. I should have known you would never do anything to draw attention to yourself."

"I'm glad you asked. Better to ask than to wonder what the truth is," he said as he took the leathers between his hands again. "It's what I've always admired about you, that you speak your mind."

She sat up a little straighter on the buggy seat and shifted Anke's weight to her other shoulder. The baby whimpered in her sleep and Honor patted her back to soothe her. "Silas always said that I was too forward for a woman. That I should think and talk less."

"I don't believe Silas and I would have had much in common."

"He was a good man, a faithful member of the church. And he was always first to lend a hand to anyone in need," she defended her husband. "He took his role as a man of our faith seriously. Isn't that what the preachers tell us a man should do?"

"Ya," Luke agreed. "But there's no harm in taking joy in it. Having a wife and young children is a great responsibility, but they can also give great joy if you let them."

"You might think differently if you had children of your own."

"I don't believe so. Think about your own father, for example. He was one to enjoy life," Luke reminded her. "I'll never forget the time he organized a trip to Delaware Bay for our school. He had us all rescuing horseshoe crabs by turning them over and letting them go back to the water. Remember how he took off his shoes, rolled up his pant legs and waded in the water with a crab net? He scooped up all those small creatures and let us see them before he put them back."

"I do," she said, smiling at the memory. *"Dat* always found a way to make whatever he did fun. Once, we had a tomato-throwing contest with rotten ones we found in the field. And he made a tire swing for me when I was really too old to be playing children's games."

"I was so sorry to hear that he passed away." Luke's voice grew husky with emotion. "Such a small thing to take his life."

Honor nodded. Sometime after Luke had moved away, her father had been helping a neighbor pull old wire from a fence around a cow pasture. Her *dat* had sliced his thumb on a nail, a puncture wound that had been slow to heal. And then, suddenly, a midnight trip to the emergency room had turned into days in the hospital and then he was dead of tetanus. Her mother had never recovered from the shock. And years later, when the doctors said she suffered a heart attack, Honor wondered if it was the loss of her mother's beloved husband that had killed her.

"It *was* a small thing to take the life of such a healthy man," she said. "And you're right. *Dat* did find pleasure in the smallest things. And he loved children, not just me, but all children."

"But you were privileged to have him as long as you did," Luke said. "I always admired your father. His only failing was his bad eye for horseflesh." He chuckled. "Remember when he bought that blind horse from Reuben Coblenz?"

She joined in his amusement. "You still remember that?"

Luke grinned. "It was only blind in one eye. But he bought the horse for a ten-year-old, and the beast had seen three times those years and had bad knees, to boot." He pulled the buggy up close to the back door. "You stay here while I go in and turn on more lights and stoke the fire. Then I'll help you get the children up to bed."

"I appreciate it," she said. "Then you should take the horse and buggy back to the mill. You can bring them home tomorrow morning." She twisted around. "Wake up, girls," she called to Zipporah and Greta. "We're here."

A short time later, Luke carried a sleeping Elijah and Justice, with a drowsy Tanner tagging close behind. He removed their coats, hats, mittens and boots, and tucked them in while Honor did the same for Anke. Ordinarily, all the children would have changed into sleeping gowns, but not tonight. They were tired, and it wouldn't hurt them to sleep in their clothes, for once.

"I feel bad sending you out into the snow," Honor said, when the teenage girls and children were all tended to and abed. She and Luke stood in the kitchen, warming themselves in front of the woodstove. "I'm serious about you taking the horse and buggy."

"Nah." Luke held his hands out to the stove and rubbed them together. "It's not that cold, and a little snow never hurt anyone. I'll put the horse up, rub him down and give him a good measure of oats. He served us well tonight, and I'll not ask more of him. Besides, I'm wide-awake, and after so much good food, the walk will do me good."

"You're certain?" She was oddly reluctant to have him leave. She should have been exhausted, but she, too, was far from sleepy. "How about a cup of herbal tea before you leave, then? It will warm you inside and…" She trailed off and picked up the kettle.

He turned to her, his face gentle. "I'd like that, Honor."

"I've apple pie, if you're interested."

"Not another bite," he protested, holding up both hands. "I'll burst. Just let me run out and put the horse up."

He was back in ten minutes, which was perfect timing because the teakettle was just whistling. He took two mugs and a bottle of honey from the shelf. "Milk?"

She shook her head.

"No, not with herbal tea, I suppose. Me, either." He

took the tea bags from a tin container labeled *Tee* and decorated with red and yellow painted tulips. "Sit," he said. "I can pour."

She did as he bade her, feeling light and a little giddy. She couldn't recall once in her marriage when Silas had poured her a cup of tea.

"I had a good time tonight," Luke said as he brought the mugs to the table. "And I think you did, too."

"Ya." She nodded. "I did." He handed her the small plastic container of honey and she squeezed some into her tea and stirred it with the spoon he'd brought for them to share. "And I'm glad you saved those people."

He took the spoon she offered and didn't answer.

She couldn't resist the barest smile. "Aunt Martha told me something else when she showed me your picture. She said that your brother ran away from the Amish to sing in a country-and-western band in Nashville."

Luke had just taken a sip of tea, and he was so surprised that he nearly choked on it. "My brother did *what*?"

She giggled. Saying it out loud made it seem all the more ridiculous. "That's what she said. I'm sure it's wrong, but…I guess I thought I should ask you for myself."

"Wait, wait." He wiped the drops of tea off his chin. "Was she talking about my cousin Harvey?"

"She said your brother."

"My brother can't carry a tune." Luke was laughing now, laughing so hard that he could hardly speak. "My *cousin* joined a Mennonite choir, when he was still *rumspringa*. Years ago."

"So, he isn't in Nashville?"

"He is not. Nor is my brother," Luke said. "Harvey, who *can* sing, is still Old Order, has a wife and five children and serves as deacon in his church."

Honor leaned forward and covered her face with her hands, suppressing another giggle. "I should have known. Aunt Martha is usually wrong with her stories, but she had the newspaper article and I thought—"

"Shhh." Luke reached his hand across the table and took hers. "It's not your fault. I should have told you about the bus accident. But I knew you were already so angry with me, I didn't... I guess I didn't want to... complicate things."

His hands were warm on hers and tendrils of excitement trickled down her spine and made her knees weak. "I'm sorry I've been so angry with you for so many years. You were wrong," she murmured. "But so was I." Her throat constricted. Long ago, when they were hardly out of their teens, she had realized she loved him. She could still remember their first kiss. "I think... I think you'd better go," she managed.

He sighed, released her hand and stood. "I should. But I'll be back tomorrow to work on the house."

"Great!" she exclaimed, looking at him over her shoulder.

"And to court you."

His words settled over her like warm rain on a summer afternoon. She turned back to him. "That's why Sara brought you here, isn't it? That was your plan from the beginning."

"*Ya.* I hoped Sara could help me get my foot in the door," he admitted. "But now this is about you and me." He exhaled. "Honor, I want to court you. It's why I came back. And you know that." He went on faster.

"Let me make what I did up to you, and give me the chance to show you that I've changed. I'm not the boy I was nine years ago."

She drew in a ragged breath, wondering if he could hear the pounding of her heart. "And I'm not that girl," she said softly.

He snatched up his coat and hat, holding them against his chest. "I love you, Honor. I always have. I always will and I think we would make a good couple. Husband and wife."

She gripped the edge of the table and rose slowly. Her legs seemed too wobbly to stand. "I can't promise anything, Luke."

He was silent for a moment. "But you'll think about it?"

Moisture clouded her eyes. "I'll think about it, but… you'll have to give me time." Then she smiled. "Go with God, Luke. Take care."

"And I'll see you tomorrow?" he asked, putting on his hat.

"Until tomorrow," she answered. There was a gust of wind as the door closed behind him and she was left alone with her doubts and fears and hopes. "Tomorrow," she whispered into the gas-lit room.

Chapter Eight

"Boys. Look at those hands!" Honor placed the sauer-braten, a time-consuming roast beef dish, on the table. She pointed with the hot mitt on her hand. "Bathroom. Wash. Now."

Luke, who was standing in the kitchen doorway, opened his hands, palms up. "I washed. Soap and everything."

Greta giggled and Honor rolled her eyes. "You know who I was talking to." She turned her attention back to her two eldest. "Justice, Tanner, move along."

Slowly the boys climbed down from the bench and made their way out of the kitchen. Honor headed for the stove to pull scalloped potatoes baked in a cast-iron frying pan out of the oven. Usually, she liked to serve the main meal of the day just after noon. But the roast had taken longer to cook than she'd expected, so they'd made do with soup and corn bread. The roast beef she'd started marinating three days ago was finally done, though supper was a full hour later than usual. Why on earth she'd decided to make sauerbraten midweek, she didn't know.

Actually, she did. She'd made it to please Luke and possibly even to show off her cooking skills. What was it that her mother used to say about *hochmut*? With pride there's always a fall? How impressed would Luke be that she couldn't plan meals or get them on the table on time? Why was she trying to impress him, anyway?

"Can I help you with anything?" Luke asked.

"Ne." She blushed, embarrassed to have been caught woolgathering. "I didn't hire you to serve meals. I hired you to fix up my house," she said, her tone a little short.

Now that Luke had moved to the mill and was working even longer hours than before, it had seemed natural to invite him to eat dinner with the family. Sometimes he even stayed for supper before starting back to the mill. She was already making a big meal, why wouldn't she share it with him?

She carried the potatoes to the table, checking to see if she'd forgotten anything. Along with the roast beef and scalloped potatoes, there were green beans, a loaf of raisin bread and stewed squash. Leftover corn bread would round out the hearty meal. She'd wanted to make a cherry pie for dessert, but there hadn't been time.

Tanner and Justice's angry voices came from the bathroom down the hall. "Boys!" Honor called. "Behave yourselves. Stop that bickering."

Justice began to wail and Honor let her hands drop to her sides in exasperation. With four children, it seemed as if *someone* was always crying.

"I'll go." Luke volunteered. And before she could say she would handle it, he was out of the kitchen and heading in the direction of the disturbance.

Honor carried the corn bread to the table, pausing to nudge a wooden giraffe out of the way with her foot.

The animal went with the toy Noah's ark Elijah had gotten for Christmas. The boys had been playing with the ark earlier, and she'd asked them to put all the pieces away. As usual, they hadn't gotten thoroughly picked up. "Elijah, put your giraffe away," she told him.

Elijah stared at the toy from his place on the bench.

Greta, already in her seat, was eyeing the corn bread.

"No eating until after grace," Honor reminded the girl.

When Greta had first arrived, she could hardly get the girl to eat enough to keep a sparrow alive, but now she ate like a blacksmith. It was a healthy thing to have a *goot* appetite. Maybe now Greta would put some meat on her bones. She suspected that meals were scanty at Greta's parents because there were so many children to feed. Thank the Lord that had never been a problem under Honor's roof.

Luke's voice rumbled over those of Justice and Tanner, but Honor couldn't make out the words. Whatever he was saying to them, it must have been the right thing because the fussing stopped. She sighed as she went to the refrigerator. She hated to admit it, but having Luke around *did* make her life easier. It was such a blessing to have another adult to lend a hand, and her boys trailed him around and pestered him instead of her. Plus, Luke had taken over milking and feeding the animals morning and night, leaving her free to do what needed doing in the house. Having an extra set of strong hands really helped on a farm.

Luke returned to the table with the two troublemakers. Both boys had apparently gotten over their disagreement because they were smiling as they climbed onto the bench and held up damp hands for inspection.

Tanner's were not as clean as Honor would have liked, but she wasn't prepared to stall her meal any longer. She'd worked too hard to put it on the table.

Luke had also worked hard for the meal and he had to be starving. Since breakfast, he'd cleaned the horse and cow stalls, replaced a rotting windowsill in the front parlor, put weather stripping around the door so that wind and snow no longer blew into the hall and applied another coat of white paint in the bathroom.

"You know the old chicken house isn't in such bad shape," Luke said once Honor had taken her place at the table and grace was over. "The boys and I could clean it, make a few repairs and move the chickens out of the barn. All you'd need is wire and staples, and I saw two rolls of stock fence in the loft. It wouldn't cost much, and the cow and horse would be a lot happier without the chickens dirtying their stalls."

"That sounds like a good idea," Honor agreed. How many times had she had to wash down the buggy before she could be seen in public? Chickens were necessary, but they could make a mess. *Like children*, she thought and then smiled as she looked around the table at her little ones.

"I can definitely get a crew together to put a new roof on, but with the weather being unpredictable, it may have to wait until April or even May. I've got supplies being delivered to do a good patch job for the meantime."

Honor noted that Luke's mention of doing the roof in May indicated he thought he'd still be around in the spring. She decided not to make a comment on that. "Whatever you think is best to keep the buckets out of my kitchen," she said.

"Honor… I was wondering," Greta said.

"Yes?" Honor secured Anke's plate to the table. The dish had a suction cup on the bottom, a useful device for keeping a toddler from throwing her entire dinner onto the floor. She handed her daughter a baby spoon. Cheerfully, Anke dropped the spoon, scooped up a handful of potatoes and stuffed them into her mouth.

"Spoon," Honor said as she put it back into the little girl's hand. "I'm sorry, Greta. What were you—" From the corner of her eye, she saw Justice slip a slice of sauerbraten off the platter and drop it on the floor. "Justice, stop feeding the dog from the table," she admonished gently.

Justice stiffened and looked straight ahead. "I'm not."

"Ith too." Elijah pointed an accusing finger at his brother. "I thaw him."

"Did not!" Justice shouted.

Honor put a finger to her lips. "Enough."

Tanner elbowed Justice, who howled in outrage.

"Boys, please," Honor said.

Baby Anke threw her spoon again. Luke's hand shot out and he caught it in midair. He handed the spoon to Honor.

"Use your spoon like a big girl," Honor said patiently as she gave it back to her daughter.

Just as Honor scooped some potatoes onto her own plate, Elijah turned over his glass of buttermilk. She jumped out of her chair to get a clean towel to clean it up, and Elijah started to cry. Justice took another piece of meat off the platter and dropped it under the table as Tanner neatly grabbed the slice of raisin bread that Greta had just finished buttering.

"Give that back," Luke instructed, pointing at Tanner with his fork.

Tanner took a big bite and Greta tried to take the bread back. In an effort to play a game of keep-away, Tanner dropped the disputed raisin bread. Before anyone could retrieve it, the dog snatched the bread off the bench and ran to the far corner of the kitchen to eat it.

"Enough!" Honor threw up her hands in exasperation. So much for a peaceful, pleasant supper. "Any more nonsense, and you can leave the table. All of you." She mopped up the spilled milk and refilled Elijah's glass. He was still crying. "You're fine," she told him, softening her tone. "Accidents happen. Eat your supper."

As Honor slipped back into her chair, Justice pushed Tanner and Tanner pushed him back. Justice reached across to take something off his brother's plate and spilled his milk into his plate. The baby began dropping pieces of sweet potato onto the floor, and while Honor was trying to pick them up, Elijah dumped half the sugar bowl onto the table.

"I'm going for my wooden spoon!" Honor went to the cabinet drawer and came back with a big spoon. She rapped it on the table. Elijah giggled.

"*Mam's* got the spoon," Justice warned, looking down at his plate.

Tanner grinned.

"What does this mean?" Honor demanded as she tapped the spoon on the table. "It means be *goot* or else," she threatened. "I *will* send you boys from this table without dessert."

She hated to have to get the spoon. She'd never threatened her children with paddling or even a tap on the knuckles. Using physical force against a helpless child was just wrong. But the sight of the wooden spoon made them consider the possibility that they just might get a spanking one of these days.

"Boys, you should all be—" Luke bit off his words, put his head down and went back to his meal.

Honor removed Justice's plate and got him another from the cabinet. "What were you going to say, Luke?"

"I'm not hungry," Tanner said. "Can I have pudding?"

"Eat," Honor told Tanner. "Otherwise, you'll be hungry when you go to bed."

"But I want rice pudding," he whined. "With raisins."

Honor grimaced. "I'm going to count to five and—"

"Flies!" Justice made a face. "You put flies in our pudding."

"I don't like flieth," Elijah wailed.

Anke shrieked with laughter and threw her spoon to the floor.

"Visiting Sunday," Greta announced. "On Sunday. Can I go?"

Flustered, Honor turned her attention to the girl. "I'm sorry. Can you what?"

"Go see Zipporah," Greta answered. "On Sunday. That's what I wanted to ask you. I could walk. You wouldn't have to take me."

"I don't know." Honor sat down yet again. She hadn't yet taken more than a single bite and she was starving. She looked down at her plate. Some of the sugar Elijah had dumped had made it to her potatoes. She'd have to eat them that way. She couldn't show the children that it was right to waste good food. "It's too far to walk in this weather," she told Greta.

"I think it would be nice if she went." Luke helped himself to more green beans.

Tanner nudged Justice with his elbow again, and Justice punched him.

"Stop that!" Honor set her fork down sharply on the table. "Hitting is wrong. You shouldn't hit your brother. Tanner, stop teasing him." She glanced back at Greta.

"I promised Zipporah I'd come see her," Greta said, staring at her plate.

"Surely you can spare her on Sunday," Luke suggested. "Greta deserves some fun."

"Let me think about it." Honor shook her head. "Three miles is a long way for a girl to walk alone." As she pushed a forkful of potatoes into her mouth, she saw Justice slide under the table and out of sight. "Justice, back on the bench. You weren't excused yet."

"If I could borrow your buggy, I could drive her," Luke offered.

"I don't eat flies in pudding," came a small, muffled voice. "Yuck."

Luke glanced under the table. "Justice, did you hear your mother?"

There was a note of irritation in Luke's voice, and Honor didn't care for it one bit. "Not appropriate. Greta isn't a child any longer," she said. The baby was starting to fuss, so she got up and took her out of the high chair. She used the clean end of the towel to wipe off Anke's face and hands and deposited her in the play yard.

"Maybe...maybe you could drive me, then," Greta suggested, meeting Honor's gaze. "Or I could take the buggy?"

"You told me you didn't know how to drive a buggy," Honor said. She shook her head when the girl's face crumpled with disappointment. "I didn't say you couldn't go. But loading all of us up and driving you to the Kings', it's a lot for me to do, Greta."

"How about this?" Luke offered, buttering a second piece of corn bread. "I'll come on Sunday and watch the boys. You take the baby and drive Greta to her friend's. You and Anke can visit with Katie at the mill or anywhere you want, and then stop for Greta when you're ready to come home."

Honor picked up her fork. "But it's a visiting Sunday. You work here all week. On Sunday, you should be visiting someone."

"I will be." Luke answered with a wink at Tanner. "I'll be visiting my favorite boys."

Tanner threw his hands up and cheered. An echo came from under the table. Anke, imitating Tanner, clapped and shrieked with laughter.

Honor saw the joy on Greta's face and couldn't resist. "*Ya*, I suppose we could do that." Her gaze strayed to Luke and she saw that he was watching her.

He smiled and she smiled back, and then she settled in to get at least a few bites of supper. Somehow, they got through the rest of the meal and things quieted down as everyone enjoyed their rice pudding.

Afterward, Luke offered to help with the dishes, but Honor refused. "You work hard enough around here," she said. "You don't need to do my work, as well. I have Greta to help me."

"And Tanner," he suggested. "He's old enough to take some responsibility."

She frowned. "He'll be a man soon enough. I think a child should enjoy being a child as long as they can."

Luke didn't look convinced. She was sure he had

something to add, but when she waited for him to argue with her, he simply shrugged and reached for his hat and coat. "I'll be going," he said. "Thank you for the meal. It was the best I've had since I can't remember when. Best sauerbraten I've eaten, for certain."

"Tomorrow I'll make pies," she promised, feeling her cheeks grow warm from his compliment. Suddenly all the planning to make the roast beef dish seemed worth it. "Sweet potato, I think. We've got a few baskets left in the root cellar, and they always turn out *goot* for me. You do like sweet potato pie, don't you?"

"Love it," Luke answered. "But then, there are few pies I don't like."

Tanner had come to stand beside her, leaning against her affectionately. "What kind don't you like, Luke?" she asked.

Luke pulled on his hat and pulled a face. "Shoofly pie. Too sweet. And too many flies."

Tanner giggled. "There's no flies in shoofly pie."

Luke glanced at the door, then at Honor. "Well, I guess I'll be going. See you in the morning. Bright and early?"

"Bright and early? What's bright and early to you?" she teased. "Justice is usually up by five."

Luke grinned. "That's a little early for me. At least, if I'm walking. It won't be a problem soon, though."

"You've found someone to transport your driving horses?"

"*Ne*, I decided to sell them. My cousin already arranged for a buyer. Charley Byler deals in horses here. He says he has a half Morgan, half standardbred mare that's good for riding or driving. And she's trained to a plow. I'm going to take a look at her on Saturday." He opened the back door. "G'night, and thanks again for that wonderful supper."

"'Night," she called. When the back door closed, everyone scooted off, and Honor cleaned away the remainder of the supper, wiped down the table, and set it with clean dishes and silverware for breakfast. She'd wanted a few moments of peace and quiet, but her thoughts weren't quiet. She kept thinking about Luke and how, even with the children's mischief at supper, she had enjoyed the day. Usually, when it was time to put the kids to bed, she was exhausted, but not tonight. Tonight she felt restless, almost wishing she'd asked Luke to stay for a game of checkers and some popcorn.

She was just sweeping the last bit of dust into the dustpan when there was a quick rap at the back door and Luke stepped into the laundry room. "Honor?"

She paused, broom in hand. "Everything okay?"

"Fine," he said. "Quick. Put on your coat and come with me. There's something I want you to see."

"Outside? In the dark?" She looked around to see if any of the children were in sight. For once, the household was quiet. She could hear Greta upstairs, singing softly to the little one and her boys were playing a game in the front room.

"Trust me. Come on." He flashed a smile that was infectious. "You'll be glad you did."

"All right," she agreed, surprised by her own impulsiveness. She set the broom aside, shrugged into her coat, wrapped a scarf around her neck and followed him out into the night. The air was cold, but the moon was out, nearly full, illuminating the frosty landscape and making the icicles that draped from the trees and the eaves of the barn and house sparkle like the dust from angels' wings.

"Watch your step," he cautioned as she hurried down the porch steps. "Everything's slippery."

"I'm fine," she answered. Her cheeks stung from the brisk air, but curiosity and excitement made her eager to see what all the fuss was about.

Together they crossed the icy yard, cut between the barn and windmill, and passed the two old apple trees, bare now of every leaf, limbs gnarled and twisted against the winter sky.

"Where are we going?" she asked.

"Shh." He caught her hand as they moved over a low spot in the meadow just beyond the old chicken coop.

Surges of warmth shot up Honor's wrist and arm as Luke's fingers tightened around her hand. She would have protested his familiarity, but her right foot hit a patch of ice and she did almost lose her footing. Luke pulled her against him and then gently put a hand on her shoulder and pushed her to a crouching position. Before she could pull free, he released her and pointed to a rise in the field.

"Ahh," she gasped. A cloud of condensation issued from her lips. Clearly visible above the winter grass, a fox—no, two of them—raced and leaped in the moonlight.

Luke smiled and put a finger to his lips.

Her eyes widened as she watched the foxes playfully chase each other back and forth over the crest of a small hill. In the moonlight, the beautiful and graceful animals were dark shadows against a silvery background. She couldn't tell whether they were the native gray foxes or the smaller English reds, but it didn't matter.

She and Luke remained there for long moments; how many, she couldn't say. Her knees cramped and her fingers grew numb from the cold, but it didn't matter. She'd been born and raised in the country, but she'd never seen such a sight. She might have remained until she suffered from frostbite if Luke hadn't caught her elbow and raised her to her feet.

"They may be at this all night," he said softly. "You should probably get inside. It's cold out."

"I'm not cold," she whispered.

The foxes must have heard their voices. One gave a sharp yip, and they halted, almost in midair, whirled and dashed away into the darkness. In an instant, the meadow was silent and as still as a painting on a January calendar page.

"Thank you," she murmured, stamping her feet to bring back the feeling. "That was…magnificent."

He chuckled. "Too good to watch alone. I thought you might enjoy it."

"I did." She glanced back in the direction of the house. "I guess I'd better get back."

"Ya," he agreed. "You should. And I should move along. I'll see you safely to the door."

She made a sound of impatience. "You think I can't walk a few hundred yards to my own back door?"

"I'm sure you can," he answered. "But just the same, I'll walk you there. I'd not have you come to harm, Honor, not for all the wheat in Kansas."

She laughed. "That's a lot of wheat. You're certain you wouldn't consider it?"

He held her arm as they trekked back, following their own footprints in the light snow. "Woman, you would argue with a bishop, wouldn't you?"

"Maybe I would and maybe I wouldn't," she teased, refusing to look up at him, even though she wanted to. "But fortunately for me, you, Luke Weaver, are no bishop."

Luke ended up getting his way about visiting Sunday. Honor left him with the three boys and drove Greta to her friend's house. Zipporah was thrilled to see her, and Zipporah's mother, Wilma, a jolly, round woman in a dark purple dress and apron, invited Honor and baby Anke to join them for the noonday meal. Honor refused, explaining that she'd be back around two for Greta. She was just turning to go when Freeman's wife, Katie, appeared in the doorway behind Wilma.

"Honor! How nice to see you." Katie stepped around Wilma and gave Honor a hug. "The girls seem to have hit it off. I'm so glad. Teenagers need friends their own age."

"Oh, just come sit for a moment, Honor," Wilma insisted, adjusting her round wire-frame glasses. "You're already here. Just long enough for coffee. We're still only half-unpacked from the move, but I know you won't judge me a poor housekeeper." She led the way into a sunny kitchen. "My Zipporah, she's so happy to make a new friend. And Katie tells me we will be worshipping together in the same church family."

"Ya," Honor agreed. "We will be so glad to have you." Anke squirmed in her arms.

"Take off that baby's coat," Wilma urged. "A few minutes won't hurt. Such a sweet little girl." She smiled at Anke and then chattered on. "My husband was glad to find this farm, such good soil with no flooding. We were near a river before, and every spring, terrible floods." She ushered them into a tidy parlor with up-holstered furniture. A cheerful fire blazed on a brick hearth, thanks to a propane fireplace insert. "Now, you just sit yourself down and make yourself at home while I fetch that coffee."

"She seems nice," Honor said when Wilma left the room.

"She is," Katie agreed, reaching to take Anke from her. "And she says her husband's brother is anxious to move here. They were in Canada before, but Wilma has relatives in Apple Grove." She took a seat on a worn green chair. "Sara's Epiphany party was fun, wasn't it?"

"It was," Honor agreed.

"I noticed you and Luke seemed to be having a good time together." Katie smiled warmly and bounced Anke on her knee. "You make a nice couple. My Freeman says Luke is a good man. He likes him. Hardworking."

"We aren't a couple," Honor hastened to correct her. "He just works for me."

Katie grimaced. "*Atch.* I'm sorry. Martha said— Never mind. You don't want to know."

Honor's eyes widened. "Don't tell me that Aunt Martha said we were dating?"

Katie chuckled. "*Ne*, she didn't. Not exactly. But to me, it looked…" She shrugged. "Forgive me. Freeman says I am too careless of what I say." She hesitated. "But I know what I know, and the way you and Luke Weaver were making eyes at each other…" She smiled. "I'm sure I'm not the only one who thought maybe where there was an understanding between you."

"But we don't," Honor protested. "I mean, there isn't. Luke and I… I knew him years ago, and…" She sighed.

"It's complicated, but *ne*, there definitely is not an understanding between us."

Katie studied her, opened her mouth as if she was going to say something more, but then pressed her fingers to her lips and rolled her eyes. "There I go again, speaking without thinking. It's your business, of course, but..." Her eyes twinkled. "If I were you, and I had such a respectable young man driving me and my children around on visiting Sundays, a candidate that Sara Yoder highly recommends, I'd give him some serious consideration."

Chapter Nine

By the time Honor arrived back at the farm that afternoon, the light was already fading and the temperature was dropping. Both she and Greta had had a wonderful day with the Kings and had followed that visit with one to the Kemps.

Anke had been on her best behavior and had been bounced and fed and made much of at one house and then the other. Now Anke had given up and fallen asleep in Greta's arms. It was too late for the baby to be napping, but there was no help for that now. She'd just have to stay up later tonight.

This had turned out to be such a nice week for Honor; for the first time in longer than she could remember, she actually felt like herself. First, there had been the Epiphany party, then her pleasant trip to Byler's for groceries and now today's visiting. She and Katie had known each other as teenagers and discovered they had much to talk about. Although Katie had no children of her own yet, she had toys for Anke to play with and seemed tickled to have a little one in her house. Honor liked Katie's mother-in-law, Ivy, and Freeman's uncle Jehu, who lived on the property. Since they all shared the same worship community, and services were to be at the mill the following week, Honor had even volunteered to come and help with food preparation the following Saturday. It had been too long since she'd done anything to contribute to lives outside her own family.

"You've been in mourning too long for one so young," Ivy had pronounced with an affectionate hug. "It's time you and your family took a more active role in the community."

Uncle Jehu had agreed. "We've got some bass in this mill pond that need catching. When spring comes, you bring those boys over. I'll teach them where the biggest fish hide. I've got a secret bait that never fails."

"My boys would love that," she'd agreed.

Her visits with Katie and with Zipporah's mother had given her a lot to think about, Honor decided as she reined the horse up near the barn. Luke had given her such a treat by watching her sons so that she could have a day for herself.

"I just hope Luke has survived the boys," Honor commented to Greta, who sat beside her in the buggy. "You know how they can be." She looked around the farmyard and was relieved not to see anything out of place. Thank God they hadn't burned the house down or dismantled the windmill while she was away. There were no chickens running loose in the yard, and for once, the donkey was quiet.

Greta nodded over the top of Anke's bonnet. "*Ya,* they can be."

Honor glanced at her. "*Can* be?"

The girl nibbled her bottom lip. "Trouble."

"Mmm," Honor agreed with a chuckle. "They are

lively, that's for certain. And I know they've given you a hard time."

"But they aren't bad," Greta assured her. "Just…just full of themselves."

Honor took a moment to consider what effect Greta's coming so far from home and being thrown into an active household might mean to a girl who'd never been away from her family. "We've been so busy lately that I haven't had time to turn around twice. But I want you to know, Greta, that I appreciate the help you've given me since you arrived. And I ask you to be patient with me. Too often, I'm quick to criticize you, instead of taking the time to show you what I want you to do."

A faint smile played over the girl's lips. "I'm glad I came," she answered hesitantly. "I know I'm not a fast learner, and…sometimes I'm clumsy, but…"

Honor shook her head. "You aren't clumsy. You're still growing. It's the way with all teenagers. And it's better to be slow than to rush into things like I usually do. You don't make nearly as many mistakes by taking things slowly."

Greta blushed with pleasure at the compliment. "I thought you weren't happy with me. That maybe you'd send me back."

Honor gently tightened the reins, slowing the horse as they came up the driveway. "Do you want to go back home?"

Greta shook her head. "*Ne.* I like you and the baby. And now I have a new friend. Zipporah."

"*Ya*, she seems like a nice girl. And in our church group. The two of you will be together often." Honor smiled at Greta. "You know, I have a nice length of lavender cloth. I'm sure we can find time to cut and pin it tomorrow afternoon, and then I can get it sewed in time for next Sunday. You're getting taller. It's time you had a new dress and apron for church. And we'll have to see about getting you some new shoes, as well." Honor glanced down. "The toes of those are about worn out."

"New? For me?" Greta beamed. "I never had a dress made new just for me before. Or new shoes. These are my sister Mary's shoes, ones she outgrew. But they were Joan's before that, so we got *goot* use out of them."

Honor was struck with a pang of guilt. *Lord, forgive me for not taking better care of this child who is in my keeping,* she thought. Why hadn't she noticed how shabby Greta's best dress was before this? Had she been so wrapped up in her own struggles that she hadn't thought about this girl's needs? Greta's parents might be hard put to keep all their growing girls in decent clothing, but she wasn't. "You'll have the dress this week, if I have anything to say about it," she promised. "The lavender will be so pretty with your fair coloring. And we'll look for some new shoes the next time we get in to Dover."

"Thank you," Greta murmured. The sparkle in her pale eyes and the red of her cheeks made her almost pretty, and Honor resolved to do more for her. The difference in their ages wasn't all that great; she might be able to think of Greta as a younger sister, the sister she'd never had and always wanted.

Arriving in the barnyard, Honor climbed down from the buggy and walked around to take Anke from Greta. Anke sighed and made small smacking noises with her lips, but didn't wake as Honor settled her against one shoulder. She was getting so heavy, growing every day.

Soon, Honor thought, Anke wouldn't be a baby any longer; she'd be a little girl.

Honor's throat tightened. She'd loved all of her babies, but this one was especially dear to her because Anke was born after Silas had passed. All children were a gift from God, but her little girl had been a special blessing. She wondered if Anke would be her last and hoped not. There was something so precious about a baby. People thought it was difficult taking care of them, but compared to mischievous boys, babies were easy.

Greta slid down from the buggy seat. "Do you want me to unharness the horse?"

"Ne," Honor replied. "It's getting cold out. Best you take Anke inside, and I'll do it."

"Shall I put her upstairs in her crib?"

"Ne." Honor shook her head. "Just put her in her play yard in the kitchen."

Just then the barn door flew open, and Tanner ran out. *"Mam, Mam,* you're back!" Behind him came Elijah. Both wore coats, hats and mittens. "We fed up the animals."

"You did?" She nodded in approval.

"Me, too!" Elijah chimed in. "Fed the animalth."

"Where's Justice?" she asked.

"In the barn. With Luke. Luke helped feed up, too," Tanner informed her proudly.

Honor chuckled. "He helped you, did he?"

"Not much," Tanner bragged. "Mostly it was us."

"Tanner puthed Juthtithe out of the loft," Elijah said.

Tanner whipped around. "Did not."

"Did."

Luke appeared in the open barn doorway. Justice followed close on his heels. "You're home." Luke smiled at her. "I was wondering if you'd make it before dark. Let me take that horse for you."

She nodded appreciatively. The wind was picking up and a few snowflakes were drifting down. She didn't want the horse to stand in the traces long after the exercise of pulling the buggy home. The animal needed to be cared for immediately and the buggy put away in the carriage shed.

"Did you have a good visit?" Luke asked as he began to unhitch the horse. "Tanner, watch what I'm doing. You're old enough to do this with a little practice."

"We did," she said and explained about her change of plans for the day. "Everything go all right here?"

Luke glanced back at her. "Nothing I couldn't handle." He hesitated. "But there was something. Maybe we could talk about it later without the little ears—" he raised a hand to cup his ear "—listening."

Honor looked down at Tanner. "What happened?"

Tanner's face reddened and he stared at his boots. "Justice fell out of the loft."

"Not exactly," Luke corrected. "Tanner and Justice were roughhousing and Tanner pushed him."

"Were you roughhousing in the loft again?" Honor turned her attention to her two oldest sons. "Did he push you, Justice?"

Justice backed up and looked down at his boots.

Honor narrowed her gaze on her eldest. "Tanner, did you push your brother out of the loft?"

"He kicked me," Tanner defended himself. "And he threw hay in my face."

With a sigh, she looked at Luke. "I'm sorry. They do this all the time. I don't approve of them fighting, but brothers—"

"Ne." Luke shook his head. "Tanner should know better than to push a younger child when they are up in the loft. He also used a pitchfork to fork hay to the cow and left it lying on the barn floor, tines up."

Honor's eyes widened and she brought a hand to her mouth. "No one stepped on it?"

"Ne. By the grace of God. But Tanner is old enough to learn that being careless with tools can cause great harm. One of his brothers could have been seriously injured." Taking hold of the horse by the bridle, Luke led it into the barn, leaving Honor with her boys.

"I didn't," Tanner protested. "He slipped and fell. I didn't push him." He sniffed and wiped his eyes with the back of his hands.

"Ya, you did," Justice whined.

Uncertain what to say, Honor glanced from one to the other. "Go in the house, all of you. We'll talk about this after supper." She clapped her hands. "Go on, now. Scoot! You, too, Elijah." She waited until they were all three inside and then followed Luke into the dimly lit barn. She'd had such a good day and now she felt terrible. "I'm sorry they were bad for you," she said.

"It's fine. They're children. And they weren't bad." Again, he hesitated. "But we did have a couple of incidents and…they need guidance, Honor."

"Ya, I agree. They do, and I try to give it to them. But Tanner isn't seven yet, and he—"

"He's old enough to know that a pitchfork can kill," Luke interrupted. "And that a fall can break an arm or a neck." He took a piece of burlap and wiped down the horse's neck and chest with strong, easy strokes.

"I think you're being too hard on him."

"I may be. But I think you're being too easy. A

woman… A mother sometimes makes excuses for her child when he should be disciplined."

"Disciplined?" Honor struggled to hold back the surge of emotion that rose in her chest. She was angry that he would interfere. But she also felt a pang of guilt. She knew that sometimes she was too easy on them, but their father had been so harsh. "What would you have me do?" she asked. "Take a switch to him? Send him to bed without supper? Tanner is a rambunctious boy. It's only natural that he'd get himself into trouble once in a while."

"Honor, listen to what you're saying." Luke's voice was patient, but it had a thread of steel that she'd never heard before. "Do you think I'm the kind of man who would use physical force on a child? I didn't say anything about punishing Tanner. What I'm saying is that you should talk to him. He's a bright boy. He has to learn self-discipline. He's older and bigger than Justice. He has to set an example for the other three."

"So you don't believe a child should be spanked?" she demanded. "Doesn't the Bible tell us that—"

"I'm not a preacher or a deacon." He stopped what he was doing and turned toward her. "I think you need to show a child what is right. And violence against anyone is never right."

"Silas didn't believe that. He thought that it was his duty to not to spare the rod."

"I'm not Silas." He pushed open the stall door. "I'm sorry, Honor. It's not my place to tell you how to raise your children. I can't imagine how hard it must be, especially since you're doing it alone. I'm not criticizing you. I think you're a wonderful mother. But what happened here today can't keep happening. You need to

make your son understand that his actions have consequences. I see how you love your children. Sometimes
being a parent means delivering a tough message."

She stared at him, and the anger she'd felt crumbled,
bit by bit. She didn't know why she'd tried to pick a fight
with Luke over corporal punishment. She didn't believe
in it, either. Mostly because she didn't think it worked.
"Silas always said I was lenient with them."

Luke shrugged. "There's a difference between causing mischief and putting someone in danger. That's
what you have to make them understand. I'm just saying this because…because I care about them and about
you." He met her gaze. "And because you know why I'm
here. You know what I want. I want you. And I want
us to be a family."

Tears sprang to her eyes. Not knowing what to say,
she turned around and walked toward the house.

Was Luke right? She couldn't help wondering if it
would be easier to be a good parent if they had a man
in their lives, a father who would make things easier
for all of them…not harder. What was the right thing
to do? With the children? And, maybe even more important, with Luke?

For several days, Honor prayed for guidance and
wrestled with her conflicting emotions concerning
Luke. Finally, she could take it no longer. Leaving Greta
to watch Tanner and Elijah, and Luke to work on patching the roof over the kitchen, she loaded Anke and Justice into the buggy and drove to Sara's house. She hoped
to find the matchmaker at home. If Sara was off somewhere, it would be a long ride for nothing, but Honor
simply couldn't ignore her concerns for another day.

To her relief, she found Sara and Ellie in Sara's kitchen making a kettle of apple butter. Sara welcomed them in, poured hot chocolate with marshmallows for the little ones and whisked Honor off to her office.

"I don't want to bother you," Honor began, but she already felt better. Sara's office was warm and cheerful with sunshine streaming in the windows, a thick braided rug under her feet and blessed quiet. The scent of apple butter cooking and almond scones just out of the oven didn't hurt, either. Sara always seemed so capable and wise that Honor's worries didn't press quite so hard on her.

"No bother at all," Sara said with a smile. She looked as tidy as a Carolina wren this morning in her dark green calf-length dress, matching apron and starched white *kapp*. Tendrils of curly dark hair framed a round face that was dominated by her strong mouth and dark eyes, which missed nothing.

Honor's hands trembled, so she steadied the cup she was holding on her knee. "I need your advice," she blurted out. "It's about Luke. Weaver," she clarified. Then she felt silly. What other Luke could she be talking about?

Sara nodded. "I thought it might be. What troubles you about him?"

"Nothing… Everything." Honor glanced out the window. There was a bird feeder. Cardinals and blue jays vied with a red-bellied woodpecker for the choice spot at the suet, while a nuthatch crept down the tree trunk searching for insects. Honor sucked in a deep breath and tried again. Why was this so difficult? "He wants to court me," she managed. "But, of course, you already know that."

"What do *you* want, Honor?"

"That's the problem." She looked back at the match-maker. Sara's attention was fixed on her, but her de-meanor was relaxed and peaceful. "I don't know what I want," Honor confessed. "He's a good man, and the children like him. I think he would be a kind father to them." She took a breath. "Kinder than their own father had been," she added softly.

"And he's an upstanding man in our community of faith."

"He is."

"Would he be a good provider?" Sara asked.

Honor nodded. She placed the mug on a small table. "He would. He…he fits all the requirements that would make him a good husband and a father—the things I told you when we discussed my finding a husband a few months ago. Luke fits well into our family. Having him there so much at the farm makes my life easier, but… but, Sara, I can't forget what he did. He abandoned me! On our wedding day! It was shameful." She couldn't meet the matchmaker's gaze as she fought tears in a rush of emotion. "He broke my heart."

Sara was quiet for a moment. "It sounds to me as if you're torn between what happened in the past and what would be the best for your future. Is that what you're saying?"

Honor rose and went to the window. She pressed her forehead against the pane and closed her eyes. "Accept-ing him, agreeing to let him court me would be the easy thing to do. And…part of me wants that. I understand why he couldn't go through with our wedding. But…my head tells me that it would be foolish to risk the same thing happening again. How do I know what's sincere and what's charm?" Hugging herself tightly, she opened her eyes and turned to face Sara. "What do I do?"

Sara took a sip of her tea. "It's true that Luke is a charmer."

"Ya." Honor nodded. "And handsome. And I know that shouldn't matter, but it does. I'd told myself that I wouldn't look for that in my next husband, but…" She let her thought go unfinished because it sounded so silly. So girlish.

Sara chuckled. "But you're human. And young."

Honor gave a little laugh. "I don't feel young. I feel middle-aged some days."

"But you're not. And your time of mourning Silas is passed. It's time to marry."

"I have to think of my children. I have to make the best choice for them. If Luke left me again, he'd also be leaving my little ones. Who are already so attached to him."

Sara got to her feet and crossed the distance between them. She enfolded Honor in her arms, and for a brief moment, Honor rested her head on the older woman's shoulder.

"Aunt Martha thinks it would cause a scandal if I allowed Luke to court me now," Honor whispered.

Sara stepped back, looking indignant. "It isn't Martha who has to make this decision. It's *you*, my girl." A smile curved her full lips, and she wiped a tear away from Honor's cheek with the tip of one finger. "Now, no more tears. Let's put our heads together and think this through."

Honor nodded and Sara waved her back to her chair.

"Drink your tea while it's hot. Black tea soothes the mind and makes any situation more bearable."

Honor sat down and forced herself to take a sip from her cup. The tea was sweet and milky and so good. "Thank you," she murmured. She fumbled for a hand-kerchief. "You must think me a ninny."

"Not at all." Sara returned to her chair behind the desk. She steepled her small hands and leaned forward on her elbows. "You already know I approve of the match. Otherwise, I wouldn't have brought him to your home. So asking my opinion doesn't make a lot of sense, does it?"

Honor shook her head and then chuckled. "I suppose it doesn't. But I don't know who else to turn to. Everyone likes Luke. They'd take his side."

"Not Martha. I've already gotten an earful from that one."

Honor couldn't suppress a giggle.

Sara smiled but then grew serious. "Have you taken your problem to God?"

"I have." Honor nodded. "I've prayed for guidance, but…God hasn't answered my pleas."

Sara rubbed her hands together. "Perhaps, or perhaps He's answered, and you haven't been listening. I believe that He has a plan for each of us. We can't see that plan and I think often we wouldn't understand it if we could." She paused. "Honor, Luke came back into your life. Some might say that makes him part of God's plan." She paused. "So I suppose my question to you is, how important is your faith to you?"

"It's everything, of course," Honor replied in a rush. "My church, my God, are everything to me. I've never doubted that ours is the true path." She gripped the cup tightly. "Or that I am a weak woman."

"Not weak, but strong," Sara corrected. "You are a strong woman, a strong mother."

"I try, but so often, I fail."

"As we all do." Sara nodded. "But if you're sincere in your conviction that God's word is the truth, then it's time for you to forgive Luke for the wrong he did you all those years ago. God forgives us our sins, and we must try to forgive those who we feel have wronged us."

"You're right. I know you're right, but it isn't easy."

"*Ne*, child, it isn't easy because we're human. It's our nature to cling to hurts and ill-spoken words. But if we expect God to forgive us, we must do the same."

Honor looked up from her tea. "I think I can forgive, but can I forget?"

"Do you have feelings for Luke? Do you think you could give him the love a husband deserves?"

"I...think so. But then I have doubts. Maybe because...because agreeing to marry Luke nine years ago was the biggest mistake I ever made in my life."

Sara shook her head. "Then you have much to be grateful for. A mistake of the heart is a small sin, not one to carry as a burden. Let it go. Set aside your anger and hurt pride, and consider Luke Weaver for the man he is today. Not the man he was nine years ago. Do you think you could do that?"

Honor gazed out the window at the birds flitting on and off the bird feeder. God's creatures. "I think I can try," she said, as much to herself as to the matchmaker. She smiled, her eyes getting misty again. "I think I want to."

Chapter Ten

The following week, Honor and the family were invited to Hannah Yoder Hartman's farmhouse for a spaghetti supper. The invitation was extended to Luke, as well. It was Hannah's husband Albert's birthday.

Luke had met Albert the previous week when he'd come out to have a look at Honor's cow. A recent convert to the Amish faith, Albert had been and remained a veterinarian to the community. Born to a family of Old Order Mennonites, he had made the change from Mennonite to Amish as easily as a gardener might slip on a pair of worn leather gloves. He'd married widow Hannah Yoder and stepped into the respected role of husband, father and grandfather in Seven Poplars.

Luke pulled the buggy up in the driveway, not far from the porch. The temperature was just above freezing and a misty rain fell.

Almost before the wheels stopped rolling, Tanner pushed open the back door to the buggy and leaped out. Elijah and Justice followed his lead.

"I don't want you tracking mud into Hannah's house," Honor cautioned. "Leave your boots on the porch when you go inside. And be on your best behavior tonight. Remember we're guests in Hannah and Albert's house."

Luke glanced at Honor with a grin. They'd had a nice ride to Seven Poplars. Honor was in a good mood and they'd chatted all the way here. Not about anything important, just life's little things. The things he imagined a husband and wife would talk about. "I think they're excited about that birthday cake."

"Maybe Zipporah's been invited," Greta said as she climbed down. "Lots of buggies." Anke threw open her arms to Greta, and Honor passed her to the girl. Greta carried the baby to the back steps and shooed the boys up and inside.

As the back door slammed shut, Luke glanced at the murky sky. "I think I'll get the horse under cover, just in case. I wouldn't want to leave him standing in the rain all evening."

Honor turned toward him on the seat and hesitantly reached out to touch him on the arm. Just a touch, and then she drew her hand back. "I wanted to thank you."

Luke smiled at her in the semidarkness. It seemed as if they hadn't had more than a moment alone all week, between bad weather keeping the boys inside and him working hard to check one item after the next off the list they created together of all the things that needed repairing on her farm. "For anything in particular?" he teased.

Her cheeks grew rosy. She was so beautiful, particularly when she blushed or got flustered. "For everything you've done. You did such a fine job patching the roof, I don't even know that I need a new one, yet."

"We'll see. In the meantime, there's a lot more to do—the siding on the house, those missing boards on the barn. And the barn definitely needs a new roof—" He broke off as a man stepped off the porch and came to greet them. "There's Albert."

The older man approached the driver's side of the buggy. "Luke! Honor! So glad you could make it. When the weather turned wet, Hannah was afraid you'd think it too far to come on a Friday night."

"Once the boys heard that there would be cake, there was no choice," Luke answered.

Albert laughed, adjusting a battered wide-brimmed wool hat on his head. "Boys do like cake. And who can blame them? Hannah's Ruth baked it, and by the size of it, you'd better all have a hearty appetite."

Luke had liked Albert from their first meeting. There was something that reminded him of his uncle in Kansas, who'd been like a second father to him. Honor was becoming friends with Rebecca and Leah, two of Hannah's daughters. Luke thought that it would be good for Honor to have more friends her own age, even if the young women belonged to the Seven Poplars church community and not her own. And he enjoyed any opportunity to escort Honor somewhere besides Byler's Store.

"I hope my children are on their best behavior tonight." Honor leaned forward on the buggy seat to speak to Albert. "They can be a little high-spirited."

"No such thing in youngsters," Albert insisted. "I say a child will be a child. Hannah and I have a bushelful of grands. The more the merrier. Nothing like a child's laughter to liven up a house full of old people." He rested a hand on the buggy door frame. "I knew your Silas, Honor. He was always one to take good care of his livestock. He never stinted on food or medicine for his cows and horses. That says a lot about a man, that he cares about dumb beasts. Too many don't, you know. I was saddened to hear of his passing. And you left alone with four little ones to care for. But we're not given to understand God's plan."

"Thank you," Honor said.

"It's true," Albert went on. "But you've done all anyone could ask, and your time of mourning is rightfully past. Silas has gone on to a better place."

Luke murmured something appropriate. Talk of Silas always made him uncomfortable.

"It was kind of you to invite us to your birthday supper," Honor replied.

"Pleasure's all ours. If it was up to me, I wouldn't have made a fuss over my birthday, but Hannah insisted. We're always pleased to welcome company, and this is as good an occasion as any. I can't tell you how pleased I was to hear that the two of you were courting," Albert continued. "Luke will make you a fine—"

"Oh, we aren't courting," Honor protested.

Albert chuckled. "Ah, like that, is it?" He nodded, smoothing his beard. "I understand." Drops of rain spattered against the buggy windshield and on Albert's hat. "Young people like to keep their privacy. Not a problem. Well, best get your horse out of the weather." He pointed toward a large barn with a sliding door standing open. "You can drive right inside. Tie up your horse, or better yet, unhitch it and turn it into a stall. Plenty of room in that barn. And don't mind the llama. Bought it to turn in with the alpacas, sort of a big guard dog, and they won't let it into the field with them yet."

"What I was saying was that you're mistaken!" Honor

called as Albert made a dash for the house and Luke flicked the reins over the horse's back. "We're not—"

"I'd heard Albert bought a llama," Luke said, ignoring what she was trying to tell Albert. "The kids would probably love to see it."

Honor turned to him. "Who told Albert we were courting?" She didn't sound angry, but she was clearly not pleased.

"Wasn't me. But someone at the mill mentioned it yesterday morning. One of Hannah's sons-in-law, I think." He chuckled. "Everyone seems to think we are."

"It has to be Aunt Martha," she muttered. "She does like to stir a pot."

He glanced at her. "So…if everyone already thinks we're courting, maybe we should be."

"Dream on," she huffed.

But something in the tone of her voice gave him hope. She didn't sound as if she was completely convinced it *was* a bad idea. Almost without realizing it, he began to whistle as he turned the horse toward the barn.

Suddenly, the rain began to come down in sheets, making it almost impossible to see, but the horse had sensed shelter and headed toward it at a trot. In no more than a minute or two, the horse and buggy passed out of the yard and into the big barn.

"Atch," Honor said. "Where did that downpour come from?"

"As my uncle used to say, it's coming down *katze un hunde*. Cats and dogs! There's a big umbrella in the back," he suggested. "We could grab that."

"I don't think the umbrella would do much good," she said, glancing over her shoulder. "The rain's blow-ing sideways. Just as well, my pie flopped. It wouldn't do to serve it wet."

Luke made no comment. Honor had made her special shoofly pie for Albert and Hannah, but somehow, she'd switched sugar for salt in the recipe. She wouldn't have discovered it if she hadn't tasted the filling before putting the pie in the oven. Unfortunately, there'd been no time to start a second pie.

Luke suspected that it hadn't been an accident and that Tanner or maybe Justice was to blame. Somehow the canisters had gotten mixed up. That was exactly the sort of trick they liked to play. They weren't mean children, but some of their antics, like removing the ladder when he was patching the shed roof, which they'd done the other day, were more dangerous than funny.

He didn't like to make assumptions when he didn't have the facts. Still, he strongly suspected that one of them had filled the sugar container with salt. Not only had Tanner been helping his mother in the kitchen at the time, but he and his brothers had found the mix-up extremely funny. But Luke didn't want to touch that subject tonight. Honor was quick to defend her children, even when their mischief got out of hand, and he didn't want to spoil the birthday outing.

Besides, it was nice being here in the dark barn, with Honor sitting beside him and rain hitting the roof and coming down outside. Cozy and intimate. He could smell the green-apple shampoo that she used. It was the same scent he'd always associated with her, because she'd used it since she was a girl. And being here, so close to Honor, he could feel that something had changed between them. He didn't know if it was the tone of her voice, the way she seemed at ease with him tonight or something too precious and fleeting to put a name to. But there was a difference, and for the first time, he was sure he had a real chance of winning her as his wife.

"A pity about the pie," Honor remarked. "I don't know how I could have done something so thoughtless as to add so much salt for sugar. The canisters in the pantry aren't even the same size."

Again, Luke bit back the urge to give his opinion on who might have been responsible. He could be wrong, and even if he wasn't, it wouldn't be his place to parent Honor's boys until after they were married. If things worked out the way he hoped, there would have to be more discipline in the household, but it wasn't something he was looking forward to tackling.

"Anyone can make a mistake," he said. "It was kind of you to think of making a pie for Albert and Hannah."

Honor sighed. "A waste of good sugar." And then she chuckled. "*Ne*, salt. Well, next time I'll be more careful."

She slid over toward the far door and he quickly got out and came around the buggy to help her down.

Other horses poked their heads over the stalls to nicker at Honor's. And then a creamy-white llama with large eyes and enormous eyelashes did the same thing only a few feet from where Honor stood. The driving horse snorted and took a few steps backward. Luke caught Honor's arm and pulled her away from the rolling buggy. "Careful," he warned. "I was afraid the wheel would crush your foot." He was afraid the llama might have startled her as well, but he didn't say that.

But Honor didn't seem in the least intimidated. "Look at it. Isn't it amazing?" She moved free from his grasp and picked up a handful of hay from the barn floor. She held it out to the llama.

"It might bite," he warned.

Honor shook her head. "No, it's gentle. Look at the eyes." She placed a small piece of timothy hay in the flat of her palm and held it out. Daintily, the creature nibbled at the treat, then carefully removed it from Honor's hand with its lips, closed its eyes and munched contently. "Good, llama. That's good, isn't it?" she murmured.

The llama bobbed its head up and down as if in answer.

"One of God's creations," Honor said. "I've never seen one this close up." And then she turned toward him, her eyes shining in the light from the buggy.

"Beautiful," he said, not thinking of the animal but of the woman standing in front of him.

She smiled at him. "We'd better make a dash for it. We don't want to make anyone wait on us. And Heaven knows what mischief the children will get in." She dusted the hay off her hands. "Maybe I will take the offer of that umbrella."

He grabbed the umbrella out of the buggy and opened it.

"It's a big umbrella," she said. "Room for both of us."

Together, they dashed through the rain to Hannah's back door. Raindrops hit him in the face and pattered against his coat, but he barely noticed. His heart was too full of possibilities and a sense that all would come right between the two of them—and that the woman he loved would never fail to surprise him.

Hannah and Albert proved as welcoming and cheerful as Rebecca had promised they would. Honor already met Leah, Susanna and Anna previously, and tonight she became reacquainted with Hannah's other daughters, Miriam and Ruth, as well as Grace, who was a Mennonite. Luke seemed to hit it off with Albert and his sons-in-law, and Tanner, Elijah and Justice quickly made new friends among Hannah's grandchildren.

Even Anke seemed to feel at home among their new friends, laughing and clapping as she was passed from one woman to another. By the time supper was over, and it was time to let the children play and the adults have their coffee, Honor felt at ease enough in Hannah's house to help Rebecca and Grace clear away the dishes and make fresh coffee.

"It's rare we eat in the big parlor," Rebecca explained, setting down a stack of dishes, "but *Mam* wanted to be certain there was room for everyone at the tables at one sitting."

Several children, including Tanner, a boy his age and a little girl in a green dress and a student's black *kapp*, dashed through the kitchen, apparently engaged in a game of tag.

"Amelia, J.J., slow down," Rebecca called. "This is your grandmother's house, not a racetrack."

"No running in the house," Honor admonished her son.

"Why don't you all go upstairs to the playroom?" Grace suggested. "I'll call you when *Grossdaddi* is ready to cut his cake. And if you see Koda, tell him that he'd better be a good boy, or else." She smiled and grimaced. "My Dakota is the dark-haired one, and he's a handful."

"No worse than Amelia," Rebecca said. "Winter's always the hardest. Caleb says you can hardly blame the kids. They have all that energy and can't get outside to run it off."

A burst of children's laughter came from the utility room, and the group trooped through again. This time, Honor counted five children, two of them hers. She wanted to tell them to go sit somewhere and find a quiet activity, but she didn't want to embarrass them in front of their new friends.

"We're a big family," Grace chimed in. She was another auburn-haired Yoder girl, with blue eyes and lovely features. Her Mennonite prayer *kapp* was smaller and her blue dress bore a pattern of tiny flowers, but she wore the same white apron as her sisters. "Keeping us straight must be confusing to those who don't know us well, but you'll soon sort us out. I'm so pleased that *Mam* and *Dat* Albert invited you to join us this evening. And I wanted to congratulate you," she said as she wiped down a kitchen counter. "I just heard the news."

Honor stooped to clean spaghetti sauce off Elijah's chin. Her boys had been surprisingly good at supper, so happy at being with a new group of children that she'd hardly heard a peep out of them from the long kids' table during the meal. "What news?" She brushed a lock of hair out of her youngest son's face and watched him dart off to find his brothers.

"Your courtship," Grace said. "You and Luke. He seems a fine choice, and he's so good with your kids."

Honor straightened and forced herself not to show her impatience. "Luke and I aren't courting," she said quietly. "I don't know where the rumor got started. He's working for me, but Luke isn't my beau and we have no arrangement."

Grace's bright eyes widened in surprise. "You

aren't?" She brought her fingers to her lips. "I'm sorry, I heard—" She glanced at Rebecca, who was dumping ground coffee into the commercial-sized coffeepot.

Rebecca grimaced. "My fault, Honor. Don't blame Grace. I'm the one who told her. We saw you together at Byler's twice, and someone told me…"

"It's okay," Honor intoned.

Rebecca rolled her eyes. "Now I'm embarrassed. I heard that the two of you are attending church services together, and we assumed that you and Luke were… Sara told *Mam* that you and Luke were a perfect match, and I thought…" She shrugged. "I am sorry."

"*Ne*, it's fine," Honor assured her. "I just wanted you both to know that it wasn't true. People keep assuming that just because—" She glanced at them. "People just assume," she repeated, feeling awkward that she was making such a fuss over the issue.

Grace chuckled. "That's what happens in a small community. We get involved in each other's lives, sometimes too involved. But, I promise, we mean well." She and Rebecca gathered up dessert dishes. "Can you grab those forks, Honor? We'd better get back to the party before we miss something."

"*Dat* Albert has a new Bible game that he wants to play before the cake," Rebecca explained. "It's something like bingo using Old Testament people and objects."

"That sounds like fun." Honor picked up the tray with the forks and spoons and followed them out of the kitchen.

Albert's game was fun, especially when everyone began shouting out when they could fill a square on their card. No one else asked about her involvement with Luke, and she relaxed and enjoyed herself. Anke crawled up into her lap and nodded off to sleep, and Rebecca showed Honor a daybed in the adjoining room, where her own baby was sleeping.

"We'll leave the door open," Rebecca whispered. "That way, we'll hear them if they make a single peep."

Hannah's daughter Susanna, and Anna's oldest girl, Naomi, gathered the other children in the kitchen with crayons, colored paper, old magazines and paste so that they could fashion homemade birthday cards for Albert. That left Honor free to join the others in the next round of bingo.

The mantel clock had just struck eight thirty when Hannah suggested that it was time to cut the cake and get the little ones home to their beds. Honor was collecting bingo cards on her side of the table when there was a loud crash and a chorus of children's shouts from the kitchen. Luke jumped to see what had happened, with Rebecca, Charley, Ruth and Hannah right behind him. Honor hurried around the table and through the kitchen hall.

"Atch," Hannah exclaimed from the kitchen. Charley erupted with a belly laugh and moved aside to allow Honor to enter the room.

Honor froze and gasped, her hands flying to her head. The door to Hannah's pantry stood open, the doorway filled with a tide of dry dog food. Buried to his knees in kibble was a wailing Elijah, and Justice was tugging frantically on his brother's arm to pull him to his feet. J.J. and Amelia stood off to the side, giggling, and a smaller child hid, wide-eyed, behind Naomi. An olive-skinned little boy with dark eyes and black hair that stood up like wheat spikes had run to help Justice and was skating on the spilled kibble.

Honor stood frozen to the spot. Elijah was yelling too loudly to be hurt, and there was indignity rather than pain in his voice. Justice was obviously unharmed. The only one not present was Tanner. Heat flared under her skin. What had her children done now? Mortification mixed with her fear that Tanner might be hurt. She tore herself from inaction and started forward, but Luke was quicker.

He scooped up Elijah, judged him sound and passed him, still protesting, to Honor. A glance at Justice sent him running out of the kitchen. "It's not a big deal," Luke said. "Just some spilled dog food. Hannah? Could I have a broom and dustpan? We'll just scoop it up and put it back in the bin. What's it got to be fifty, sixty pounds, maybe? We'll have it cleaned up in a jiff."

"Tanner?" Honor called, wondering where he had gotten to. She clutched Elijah against her and gently bounced him. "Hush now, Elijah. Hannah, I'm so sorry."

Hannah laughed. "I told Albert it was silly to store that kibble in one big can. He got a good deal on broken bags at the store, and he insisted none of it go to waste. Someone's always dropping strays at our farm. He makes certain they're healthy and well mannered and then finds them homes. I think we're feeding five dogs now."

"Seven, *Mam*," Rebecca corrected. "The one had two puppies this morning." She nodded to Luke. "The cake is on the top shelf." She pointed. "Do you think you could pass it to me?"

"No problem," Luke said, wading through the kibble. He took the large cake off the top shelf and gingerly made his way back to the pantry doorway, where he passed it to Rebecca.

Just then, Tanner popped up from behind a table in the pantry and darted for the doorway, sending dog food flying.

Honor reached for him but he slipped past her and ran through the kitchen, toward the parlor.

"I'm so sorry," Honor repeated to no one in particular. She put Elijah down, and he followed his brothers.

Ruth and Charley each returned with a broom and a dustpan. "I'll help Luke with cleanup," Charley said. "No need to worry."

"Let's leave them to it," Hannah declared. "Capable hands." She waved her family and guests back into the parlor. Ruth brought the coffeepot, and Rebecca, the cream and sugar.

"What was all the fuss about?" Albert asked when they all returned to the table.

Hannah laughed. "Kibble. Somehow, the bin of kibble tipped over. But your cake is fine."

"A good thing I put it up high," Ruth said.

They hadn't finished the first cup of coffee when Luke and Charley joined them, Charley carrying the cake decorated with a hand-carved wooden llama and a circle of candles.

"If that thing looks more like a goat than a llama, don't blame me," Charley said.

Everyone laughed and admired the cake.

"Your pantry is restored," Luke declared. "The dog food is all back in the bin with the lid on tight, and every piece accounted for."

"Not every piece," Charley teased. "I think Luke ate a couple."

Luke laughed. "That was you, Charley."

"Exactly *what* happened to my dog food?" Albert asked.

"Some of the children, who shall go unnamed—" Luke glanced at Honor and she mouthed a silent thank-you "—were admiring the cake from the top of the kibble can. The can tipped over and..." He spread his hands and chuckled. "The rest is history."

Laughter rippled around the table. "If Charley wasn't in here when the bin went over," Ruth said, "I would have suspected him. His mother told me he once fell into a barrel of pickles."

"He must have smelled like a dill pickle for weeks," Anna's husband, Samuel, said before topping all the stories with his tale of spilling a bucket of maple syrup in the middle of a church service at the bishop's house.

Someone lit the birthday candles, and family and guests joined in to sing "Happy Birthday" to Albert. Cake was enjoyed by all, coats and hats were found, babies were bundled up and men went out into the night to hitch up the horses.

When Honor carried a sleeping Anke to the buggy and made certain Greta and the boys were safely inside, the worst of her embarrassment had passed. Hannah and her daughters hugged Honor and told her again how happy they were that she'd come, and Albert told her to come back anytime.

The rain had let up, and a sliver of a moon peeked out between the clouds as Luke guided the horse down the country road. With the children and Greta in back, Honor was all too conscious of the strong male presence beside her.

They were almost home before she finally spoke up.

"It was wonderful, what you did for me tonight," she said quietly. "For my children. Cleaning that mess up. Thank you."

He chuckled. "It was a lot of dog food, wasn't it?"

"I suppose Tanner was the culprit."

"Possibly." He looked down at her. "I think you'll have to ask him that tomorrow."

"The two oldest know better."

Luke smiled in the darkness. "There was no harm done."

"But they're mischievous," she said, feeling guilty again. "And I told them to be on their best behavior." Would Hannah think she was a bad mother for not demanding answers on the spot? For not punishing them? For not even making them clean up the mess? Was she? She hadn't known what to do. She still didn't. But Luke had. Luke had come to her rescue. She sighed. "You are an amazing man, Luke Weaver," she said.

"Isn't that what I've been telling you?" he replied.

And they laughed together.

Chapter Eleven

Honor glanced up from her sewing machine to the mantel clock. The morning had slipped away as quickly as most days did. She'd fed the children, cleaned up the breakfast dishes, washed and hung clothing on the line, baked biscuits, put a chicken in the oven to roast for the midday meal and had churned some fresh butter to spread on the bread.

She did make good butter, she had to admit that. Good butter making was a gift. Not every woman possessed it, but she wasn't showing pride in acknowledging that hers was worthy of praise. Nothing that came from the store tasted as rich or as sweet. Luke had even said as much to Hannah at the birthday supper.

She'd had such a good time that evening. In spite of the mischief with the spilled dog food, she'd enjoyed herself. It was wonderful to be able to get out of the house and make new friends, but most of all, being with Luke—having him come to her rescue—had warmed her heart.

He seemed to know instinctively what to do with her boys. And, in doing so, he lifted a heavy weight off her shoulders. For the first time in her life, she felt that she wasn't alone in the responsibility for her children. It was silly, of course. She and Luke had no commitment to each other. Hadn't she told him that he was only here on her farm to work? She'd implied, if not said directly, that there was nothing between them and never would be again. The question was, did she believe that anymore? Had she been able to do what Sara had suggested? Was she letting go of the past and looking at the future?

She looked back at the half-stitched seam on Tanner's new trousers. A few more minutes and she could finish. He was growing as fast as a pokeweed. Sometime this winter, her precious little son had sprouted into a long-legged colt. His wrists were shooting out of his sleeves, and his trousers were suddenly bursting at the seams, too short to wear in public.

All three boys were outside, watching Luke repair the windmill, and Anke was napping. Greta was setting the table for dinner and keeping a close eye on the chicken. The previous afternoon, the two of them had made applesauce with apples that were growing soft and prepared potato salad. Earlier, she'd sliced carrots and onions to roast with the chicken, so putting the noon meal together would be a snap. She knew that she should put up the sewing and summon Luke and the children to the table, but quiet was rare in this household. She'd always enjoyed sewing, and she savored her time alone to think while her hands were busy.

She felt as if she had to make a decision about Luke. The thought had been nudging her for days. Should she agree to allow him to court her, as Sara so obviously wanted? Or should she send him on his way, as

Aunt Martha had urged her? She knew that she needed to make up her own mind. That was the problem. She didn't know her own mind. Luke seemed to be the answer to her prayers and to the empty place in her heart. But…

What if she couldn't let go of the hurt he'd caused? Maybe the small voice in her head that urged her never to trust him again was the voice of reason. But sending him away now? Could she do that? Could she be certain that another man would fit into her family so easily? Would she ever feel the kind of connection she felt with him?

God forgive her for thinking ill of the dead, but she and Silas had not been compatible. He had been a good man, but from the beginning, they had rubbed on together like a mismatched team of oxen. No matter how she bowed to his position as head of the house and father of her children, her heart had secretly rebelled. And she had done him a disservice by never loving him fully, as she should have done. Would it have made a difference? In time, would her desire to have a good marriage have won out over her own willfulness? She didn't know, and now she never would.

She pumped the pedal and carefully guided the material to finish the seam. She snipped off the thread and held up the blue trousers for inspection. She'd allowed for a wide hem, and that she could stitch up tonight after the youngest ones were in bed. She'd have the pants ready for Tanner to wear tomorrow. His best ones could go to Justice in the fall, and she had enough of the blue cloth left to make a second pair. Smiling, she turned the trousers right side out and had begun to fold them when her peace was shattered by a child's scream. The kind that terrifies a mother.

By the time Honor reached the yard, Greta was already there and had added her wails to those of Elijah. Tanner's face was white, and Justice stood with tears running down his cheeks. His mouth opened and shut but not a sound came out.

"What is it?" Honor demanded. She looked up at the windmill, but didn't see Luke. "Is someone hurt?" she asked. The temperature had risen sharply since the wet night they'd gone to Hannah's, and the ground was muddy. Water squished around Honor's shoes and soaked her stockings. Bewildered, she looked from one to another, and then she reached Tanner and gripped his shoulder. "What happened?"

He pointed toward the board fence that separated the barnyard from the field. "Luke fell," Tanner said in a thin voice. "He fell and…" Sobs wracked his small body. "He's dead. Luke's dead."

Honor stared at her son, frozen for a moment. "Don't say that," she admonished. "That's not funny. You don't make a joke about—" Suddenly, she had no breath left in her. Darkness threatened to envelop her. Dead? Luke dead? Impossible. What was the child saying? Gooseflesh rose on the back of her neck and prickled the skin on her arms. "Luke fell?" It came out a whisper, but Tanner nodded, still pointing toward the fence.

And then she saw a man's foot encased in a black high-top shoe on the far side of the bottom rail. Somehow she closed the distance in a heartbeat and climbed the fence. Hatless, Luke lay sprawled on his back in the mud. His arms were flung out on either side of his head, his legs as motionless as if they were carved of wood. Luke's face was as pale as bleached flour, his eyes closed.

"Luke?" She fell to her knees beside him in the mud, and her blood turned to ice. Luke appeared to be asleep. His waxen lips were parted slightly, and his features were smooth. He'd shaved this morning, and she noticed a tiny scratch where he'd cut himself along his jawline. She could smell the clean scent of Ivory soap on his skin. "Dear God," she whispered. "Let this be a bad dream." She pressed her palm against the side of his throat, trying to find any sign of breath. "Luke," she murmured. She turned to look at Tanner. "He fell? How far? Off that?" She pointed at the windmill.

Tanner nodded. "From the top."

Honor tried to shut out the sound of the children's cries as she tried to figure out what to do. Was Luke broken beyond healing? Had the fall snapped his neck? His back? She touched his cheek. The noonday air was cool and moist, but his skin seemed chilled. "Luke," she repeated.

She didn't know what to do. She pressed her fingers to his throat again. She thought she could feel a pulse, but what if she was wrong? If only she had a phone. But the nearest telephone was at an English neighbor's house, too far to send Tanner on his own to call for help. Sending Greta would mean leaving the baby alone in the house for too long.

"Luke!" She patted his face again, first gently and then harder. "Luke!" If only she hadn't lingered over her sewing. If only she'd called them to dinner five minutes ago. If only… The enormity of her loss washed over her in waves. Luke was dead and she'd never told him that she loved him. "Don't be dead," she whispered.

"He's dead, isn't he?" Greta peered between the boards, her eyes wide and frightened.

"He's not dead," Honor insisted. He couldn't be. It was impossible that someone could have been laughing and teasing her only an hour ago and now lying lifeless in her corral. Desperately, she placed her fingers over his lips, praying for some sign of breath.

Nothing.

"Luke," she ordered. "Wake up. Wake up, Luke." She bent and brought her own lips close to his. Did she feel... *Ya?* Her heart hammered against her ribs. Surely it wasn't her imagination. She'd felt something, hadn't she? "Luke?" She seized his shoulders and shook him. "Wake up!" What was it her grandmother had told her about reviving a grandchild who had fallen off the barn? "Greta! Bring me a bucket of water! Now!"

She studied Luke's face. No movement. Not so much as a muscle twitched. Not an eyelid fluttered. Time passed. Seconds? Minutes?

Greta dropped a sloshing bucket into the mud beside her. Honor looked from the clear water to the mask that was Luke's face and back again. "Please, God," she whispered as she dashed the cold liquid over him.

Luke gasped. His eyes flew open, and he coughed. He tried to sit up and then fell back into the mud. His eyelids fluttered, and he drew in a long breath.

"You're alive," Honor whispered.

He groaned. "I think so." He exhaled slowly. "Did I..."

She nodded, wanting to shout, to throw herself onto him and to kiss him. "We thought you were dead," she managed. She used her apron to pat the water off his face. Tears ran down her cheeks.

"So you tried to drown me?" His voice came low and

rasping, but his eyes focused on her face and the corners of his mouth turned up in a crooked smile.

"You fell from the windmill," she managed, finding suddenly that she could barely catch her breath. She wanted to cover his face with kisses, to hold him in her arms. She clasped her hands together to keep from touching him. "I think you should lie still. You might have broken bones."

He groaned again and flexed first one limb and then another. "I don't think so." He sat up and put his hands on either side of his head. "The board broke," he said. "The one I was standing on. I didn't want to fall on the concrete pad or the fence. I think I jumped."

Shakily, Honor got to her feet. "Greta, take the little ones into the house. Make certain everything on the stove is turned off. Tanner, see if Anke is awake. If she is, you can get her out of her crib."

"He's not dead?" Tanner asked.

Luke scoffed. "Do I look dead?"

"I think you should stay where you are." Honor fretted. "You may have a concussion. Or you could have internal injuries." She turned to Greta. "Please see to the children."

As Greta rounded up the boys and led them away, Luke slowly got to his feet. "Nothing's broken. I'm fine. Just a little woozy." He took a step and staggered. Instantly, she was at his side, supporting him.

"In here." She helped him into the barn through the open doorway. "Sit," she ordered when they reached a bale of straw. "Even if you didn't break your neck, you've taken a bad fall. You probably knocked your brains loose."

"I'm fine," he repeated, but he did as she told him

and sat. "The mud absorbed most of the blow…when I hit."

With her hopelessly muddied apron, she dabbed at his face again at the smears of dirt that streaked his cheeks. He'd lost his hat in the fall but that didn't matter now. "You're alive," she murmured. "I thought… I thought…" And then she lost whatever control she had and began to weep great sobs of relief. Tears blurred her vision, so that she was only vaguely aware when he stood again and put his arms around her. "I thought I'd lost you," she wailed. "And I hadn't told you—" She took a deep, gulping breath.

"Shh, shh," he soothed, rocking her against him. "You hadn't told me what, Honor?"

The words *that I love you* rose to her lips, but she couldn't utter them. Instead, she laid her head on his shoulder and drank in the strength of his arms and the blessed sounds of his breathing. It wasn't too late, she realized. God had given her a second chance. "I think," she began and then found herself racked by another sob. "I think I would…like to…"

"Like to what?" He patted her shoulder. "Don't cry, Honor. Please don't cry. It's all right. I'm all right. Tell me."

"Luke, I think we should… I want to…" She wiped at her tears with a muddy hand, trying to find the words.

He searched for a handkerchief, but when he pulled it from his pocket, it was as wet as his coat and trousers. She stared at it, and her sobs became gasps of laughter.

Soon, Luke was laughing with her. "Is this your way of saying you'll marry me?" he asked. "Is that what you're trying to say?"

"Ya." She nodded, pulled free from his embrace and

wiped her eyes with the backs of her hands. "If you still want…"

"Say it," he urged. "Say the words."

She covered her face with her hands and then sniffed. She glanced down at her apron and skirts. Her muddy stockings sagged around her ankles, her shoes were soaked and her apron was dirty beyond belief. "*Ne*. You have ask me properly, first," she said, sniffing again.

"I'll ask you a hundred times if I have to."

He smiled at her, and her chest felt tight. She'd come so close to losing him. In those terrible minutes when she'd thought he was dead, all her doubts had evaporated, and all she could think was how much she needed him. Not only her, her children needed him. "My Anke… My boys need a father," she whispered.

"And I want to be that father. I want to be your husband. So will you let me court you?"

"*Ne*." She shook her head, fighting another wave of tears. She was so thankful for God's grace. "I don't need that. We've had our courtship, Luke. I think that's what we've been doing here these last weeks." She looked up at him. Took a breath. "I want us to marry…as soon as possible. I don't want to be alone anymore. And you're the only man I want, I'll ever want for my husband."

Now it was Luke whose eyes glistened with emotion. "I prayed I could win your love again. I was certain that God meant for us to be together. But I nearly lost faith that it could happen. But now God has answered my prayers. I'll be a good husband to you, Honor. I will be the best father to your children…to *our children* that I can."

"It was my foolish pride that kept us apart," she said. "But I never… Luke, I never stopped loving you."

He caught her hand and gripped it. "I love you," he said. "I've loved you since I was eight years old and you threw that ladle of well water on my head."

She laughed. "And now I've done it again, but this time with a whole bucket."

He turned her muddy hand in his and pressed his lips softly against the underside of her wrist. "If I'd known it would win you over, I'd have jumped off the windmill the first day I got here," he said.

He tugged at her hand, and she knew that in another second she'd be in his arms and he'd be kissing her mouth. And she wanted him to. But she made herself pull away from him. "First, we see you to a doctor and then to the bishop," she said. "I think it's wise we marry soon."

"The sooner the better," he agreed. "As soon as the *banns* can be cried."

She nodded, backing away from him. "I do love you, Luke Weaver," she said, and then she whirled around and ran for the safety of the house and her children.

"I haven't done this since I was sixteen," Honor said to Luke, holding on to his arm for balance. "I'll probably fall and break my neck."

"Skating isn't something you forget," he assured her.

She sighed. "I hope you're right." After a final glance over her shoulder at the campfire where members of the Seven Poplars youth group were helping her boys roast hot dogs, Honor made her way cautiously out onto the ice. Luke sat down to lace up his skates, and she took the opportunity to practice a few easy moves.

So much had happened in the past week that she could hardly believe it. Luke had gone to her bishop for permission for them to marry, and they were only waiting for certification from his Kansas church community to set a date. Most Amish weddings were held in November and December, but as a widow, she could marry at any time.

The only bad thing was that the bishop had asked Luke to stop working on her house until after the wedding, unless accompanied by others who could serve as chaperones. Since they'd made it plain that they cared for each other, the elders felt that the less time they spent together until they became man and wife, the more respectable it would appear to outsiders.

Honor could understand the bishop's decision, but she did miss having Luke at her table, and the children asked for him every day. Being with him tonight was even more special because he'd been absent all week. Typical of Delaware weather, the thaw hadn't lasted. The temperature had dropped to the single digits and the ice on the millpond had frozen faster and harder than it had in years.

"I thought you said you'd forgotten how to skate." Luke called, coming up behind her on his skates. "Race you to the far side."

Her response was to lengthen her stride, and she glided away from him. It felt wonderful to fly along on the ice with the wind on her face and the full moon illuminating the pond as brightly as twilight. Birds must feel like this, she thought. It was a glorious night, and her *grossmama* Berta's old skates fitted her as though they'd been made for her.

Honor and Luke had skated before, one cold winter when they were first dating, years ago. Tonight, it was almost as if those years had faded and she was young again. The moon was huge and bright, and the ice a sheet of silver. She could smell the crackle of apple wood on the fire and hear the sounds of children's laughter rising above the hiss of the skate blades. She felt as light as a feather…as free as a puff of wind as they skimmed over the frozen millpond. How could she have forgotten how much she loved Luke…how happy he made her?

Other Amish families and couples had gathered along the wooded shoreline of Freeman's pond, glad for an opportunity to get together for an evening of fellowship and pleasure. Anke was safely in the house with Katie and some of the women, and Greta and Zipporah were helping serve hot chocolate and marshmallows. A few Amish were on the ice, some with skates and some with sleds or just sliding along on their shoe soles, but she and Luke had most of the expanse of the large pond to themselves.

They reached the opposite bank side by side. She turned to avoid a tree root jutting out of the earth and spun out, landing on her bottom and sliding across the ice. Luke was immediately at her side, getting down on his knees beside her. "Are you hurt?" he asked.

She shook her head and laughed. "*Ne*, just feeling silly. Pride goes before a fall."

His gloved hand closed around her arm and he leaned close. "Do you have any idea how beautiful you are tonight?"

"*Don't,*" she protested, but hearing him say so was sweet.

"Kiss me," he said.

"*Ne.*" She shook her head, savoring the giddiness

that made her tremble. "No kissing until we're man and wife."

"Just one kiss?"

His voice was teasing, but she found herself staring at his mouth. Wanting to press her lips to his. "*Ne*, absolutely not. We're not teenagers, Luke."

He groaned. "Honor, Honor, Honor. You're right, but..." He sighed and got to his feet. He offered his hand, and she took it and he pulled her up. "Skate with me," he said.

"All right." She felt her left skate suddenly loosen. "Wait," she said. "I think my lace came undone."

Still holding her hand, Luke helped her to the edge of the pond. "Here. Sit here," he said, motioning to a section of a tree that lay half below and half above the ice. She did as he told her, careful to keep her skirt in place over her thick stockings.

"Let me see your skate."

Her heartbeat quickened as he took her skate in his hands and bent over it.

"Ah" He nodded. "The lace snapped. I think I can knot it so it will work."

She breathed in the cold, clean air with its bite of cedar and pine. She could see the others on the other side of the pond and she assumed they could see her and Luke, but here in the quiet semidarkness, it seemed as if they were alone in the world beneath this silvery moon.

He pulled off his gloves and unlaced her skate. "The rest of the lace seems strong enough," he said. He knotted it just above the break and then laced the top again, leaving an inch-long gap between. "If it doesn't hold, I can give you one of mine," he offered.

"Let me try. It feels all right," she answered. "We should go back to the group, anyway."

But she didn't want to go back. She wanted to go on skating alone with him, with her heart full and his strong hand clasping hers. Was it wrong to feel like this? She was a widow, a mother of four, but this couldn't be wrong, could it? She shifted her weight and skated a few feet beside him. "I think it's fine," she said.

And then they were off again, hand in hand, skimming over the shimmering surface, finding joy in being together and silently making promises to each other about the days and months and years ahead.

Chapter Twelve

"Boys, you're too noisy. Go outside and play. Better yet…" Honor stopped pedaling her sewing machine and looked up.

Freeman's mother, Ivy, had come to visit while her son helped Luke out with a project. While Honor worked at her sewing machine, Ivy was knitting. The two women had been trying to talk when the boys got too loud. "Get your coats on and go watch Luke and Freeman repairing the chicken house. Learn how it's done, so that you can mend your own buildings someday. They might even find work for you to do."

"We want to skate," Tanner said. "Can you take us to the millpond? I'm going to take my sled."

"Ne," Honor replied firmly, glancing down as she lifted the pressure foot of the sewing machine. "I've no time to take you anywhere today. We can't play on the pond, anyway. Freeman says the warmer temperatures are melting the ice."

Tanner pulled a face. "But we wanna go. We could stay close to the bank." Justice stood solidly behind him, the two of them united in a purpose for once, instead of quarreling or teasing each other.

Honor removed the shirt she was sewing and shook it out. "You heard me," she said. "Skating is only safe when it's very cold and the ice is thick. It may freeze again this month, or we could have to wait until next winter. We'll just have to wait and see."

"But we want to go," Justice insisted.

Honor took a deep breath and prayed for patience. Since the night of the winter frolic the previous week, Tanner and Luke had been wild to return to the mill with their sled. But the changeable Delaware weather made skating a rare treat. Some winters the temperatures never dropped and held long enough to make ice-skating safe at all.

"Please," Tanner begged.

"You heard me," Honor replied, becoming slightly embarrassed that the boys were being difficult in front of company. "The two of you go outside and play in the yard." She studied the shirt collar carefully, trying to decide if the seam was perfectly straight.

Justice looked pitiful. "But there's nothing fun to do in the yard," he said.

"What you both need is something useful to do," Honor replied. "See if you can figure out where the white hen is hiding her eggs."

Tanner shook his head. "She pecks."

"And scratches," Justice argued. "We should put her in the pot and eat her."

Honor didn't want to scold them in front of company, so she forced a cheerful expression. "The white hen is a good egg producer," she explained brightly. "And she'll raise baby chicks for us in the spring. She's an excellent mother."

"I'll gather the eggs," Greta offered, coming into the kitchen. She crossed the kitchen and reached for her heavy shawl. "Come on, Tanner. Justice." Reluctantly, the boys trudged after her to put on their coats.

Honor returned to the table, where Ivy was knitting a blue baby cap. "It rained all day yesterday, and they've got so much energy that they get restless when they stay inside."

Ivy smiled and nodded. "I know about little boys and big ones. It's a pity about the ice. Freeman's father was very strict about the pond. When Freeman was little, he would beg and beg to be allowed to skate, but we never let him unless the pond was frozen from bank to bank. The ice must be two inches thick, and it's nothing like that now."

With Ivy there, not even the bishop could complain about Luke being on Honor's farm if they were chaperoned by such respected elders. And Honor liked Ivy and was glad for her company. She reminded Honor of her Grandmother Troyer, now passed on and greatly missed.

The men had carried Honor's sewing machine out into the kitchen so that the women could be at the center of everything while they did their needlework. It was so nice here, with the sun coming in the windows, that Honor thought she might move some of the furniture and keep the sewing machine there until spring.

"I hope Elijah's cold doesn't get any worse," she said to Ivy. Elijah had had the sniffles for several days and was cutting a molar, so after listening to his whining, Honor had tucked him back into bed at the same time she'd put Anke down for her nap. He protested for about ten minutes and then dropped off to sleep. She'd made chicken soup the previous day and had hoped some hot soup and plenty of rest would set him as right as rain. Her children were rarely ill and she hoped the rest of them wouldn't catch the toddler's cold.

"So long as your Elijah doesn't develop a fever or a bad cough, I think he'll be fine," Ivy commented. "He's a sturdy little one. And you're so sensible with him. You should have seen me when Freeman was small. If he sneezed, I was driving him to the doctor. Once, I took him to the emergency room for an infected mosquito bite." She sighed and smiled from under her black elder's *kapp*. Ivy's face was surprisingly unlined, and her eyes were bright. "He was our only one, you see," she said. "The only one who lived. And I was constantly in a panic that something would happen to him." She beamed. "But God blessed us, and he flourished in spite of my fears. Look at the size of him now, grown to a big, hearty man."

Honor paused from sewing a button on Tanner's spring jacket. Her heart went out to Ivy, having only one child and being unable to have any more. Honor couldn't imagine what she would do if anything happened to one of her four. Or the ones she and Luke might be blessed with… Her children were her life, and the truth was, she was looking forward to a bigger family. God willing, of course.

She swallowed and glanced around the kitchen. Soon Luke would be sharing her life permanently. He would help her with the farm and with the children. A small shiver of excitement spiraled up her spine. And with it came an icy thread of doubt.

"Ivy?"

"Ya?" The knitting needles paused, and Ivy rested them and the cap on her black apron.

"Do you think I'm marrying again too soon?" That wasn't what she wanted to ask. She wanted to ask Ivy if she thought that Honor was being foolish. Because she felt foolish. At times, she was downright giddy. There was no other word for it. She was giddy over Luke and the thought of making a life with him. Once, all those years ago, they'd shared a kiss behind the schoolhouse on the way home from a singing. She still remembered that kiss, dreamed about it…

"Why would you ask that?" Ivy said. "Of course not. A decent time has passed since Silas was laid in the earth. I've known women with children to marry again before the first year was up, and few thought to criticize them. A woman is meant to be married, and children are meant to have a father. It's God's way. It's our way."

"We nearly married before," Honor admitted. She wondered how much to reveal about Luke, but she felt the need to talk and Ivy seemed open to listening. "Before I agreed to become Silas's wife. But we… Luke and I… broke it off."

"I know about that," Ivy said with a wave. "Your almost marriage to Luke was common knowledge around the county. Yours was a different church community, but talk gets around. And don't think you two are the first or the last couple to call off a marriage at the last moment. Sometimes it's the wisest thing to do."

Honor looked down at her hands, now still. "It was Luke's doing, not mine."

"But you were both very young. Too young, some would say. I think a woman needs to be in her mid-twenties to know her own mind when it comes to marriage. Most women. I know that I would have been far too unsteady to have married sooner. Too much a girl to make a good wife if I'd married before I did. Marriage is hard. You have to put the other person first. We waited to exchange our vows, and it was worth it. He's gone now, my first husband, but a better man never walked God's earth. And I counted my blessings to have him. And now to have my Jehu. God is good."

"So, you don't think I'm rushing into this? With Luke? My aunt Martha does. She's against it. She thinks we'd be a terrible match."

Ivy glanced up from her knitting and chuckled. "Martha disapproves of a lot of things, but no one's asking Martha to marry Luke." Her eyes twinkled. "This has to be your decision, Honor. And Luke's. Not mine and certainly not Martha's. Besides, Sara Yoder thinks you've made a good match, and she's a sensible woman. And so is Hannah. She's so taken with you and Luke, she tells me that she's offered to have your wedding at her home."

"She did, but Sara offered first. It was so sweet of Hannah to offer, but we've decided to hold the ceremony at Sara's. The bishop is just waiting for a letter from Luke's church confirming his baptism. We want Katie and Freeman to be part of the wedding party, and Sara's already planning the menu. You'd think I was her daughter instead of just a client."

"You're more than a client," Ivy assured her. "You know Sara never had any children of her own. She thinks of all of her brides and grooms as her sons and daughters. She says so all the time." Ivy chuckled. "Sara may seem tough, but inside, she's as soft as new butter."

Honor nodded, reassured. She finished the last

stitches on the shirt collar and then got up to check the roast. She was planning on making buttered noodles, a green bean casserole and scalloped potatoes for the mid-day meal. Ivy had brought a coconut cake and canned spiced pears to go with dinner.

Greta came in with the eggs. "Only eight today," she said.

"Are the boys staying out of Luke and Freeman's way?" Honor asked, reaching for hot mitts.

Greta nodded. "They hitched up the donkey to the sled and were driving it around the field." She removed her bonnet and retied the ends of her headscarf. "Want me to check on Anke?"

Honor nodded. "And would you make certain that Elijah is covered? He's as wiggly as a goat. Half the time his blankets end up on the floor. I wouldn't want him to take a chill." She slid the pan of scalloped potatoes into the oven. She felt a little better after talking with Ivy. She supposed that every woman must be nervous about a coming wedding. Marriage was a serious matter. God willing, she and Luke would be married for the next fifty years.

She loved Luke, she was certain of that. And she believed that he would make a good father for her children. It would be all right. They would be all right. In just a few weeks, she would stand before the bishop with Luke and they would be man and wife. She was scared, but in a good way, and the sooner they could make their promises to each other, the better for her and for her children.

It was a little after one o'clock when she finally had the food on the table and stepped out on the back porch to ring the dinner bell. "Come and eat!" she called.

The air was brisk, but the sun was shining. She judged it to be in the forties, not a bad day for February. She ran the bell a second time, and Luke and Freeman appeared at the far end of the yard.

She smiled to herself. How fine Luke looked, with his tool belt around his waist and shoulders wide and strong. He wasn't quite as tall as Freeman, but Honor's throat warmed at the sight of Luke and his friend striding toward her. She wasn't alone anymore. She had a good man who wanted to marry her and she had friends. Truly, she felt blessed.

She didn't see the boys, so she rang the dinner bell yet again. "Have you seen Justice and Tanner?" she called to Luke. "Are they coming?"

The two men drew closer. "Haven't seen them in a good while," Luke replied. "They had the sled hitched to the donkey and were taking turns riding around the field."

"I saw them," Freeman said. "An hour ago, maybe more. They were going down the lane. I thought maybe you'd sent them to pick up the mail from your box."

Honor went to the far corner of the back porch and looked down the driveway. There was no sign of her boys. "Maybe they're in the barn," she said, hoping that they'd tired of their game and put the donkey in his stall. She pulled the rope again, and the old bell pealed.

"I'll go look," Luke said. "They can't have gone far."

"You know how kids are," Freeman said. "When they get playing, they forget everything else, even dinner."

When Luke came striding back alone, Honor's throat tightened. A shiver became a chill, despite the fact that she now had her cloak on. "Is the donkey there?" she asked. He shook his head, and suddenly she was afraid. "They've gone to millpond," she said. "Tanner wanted me to take them. He was going to take his sled to play on the ice."

"*Ne*, I don't think they'd do that. They've never gone that far before, have they?" Freeman's expression darkened. "The ice on the pond has been melting."

Honor's hand flew to her mouth. "That's where they've gone. I know it. Luke, hitch up the horse for me." She came down the steps toward him. "We have to get to Freeman's. Katie's not home today. There would be no one there to send them home."

"You really think they'd go to the millpond? By themselves?"

She nodded, starting across the barnyard. "Once Tanner gets something in his head, he doesn't let go of it. I've got to go after them before something terrible happens." If Tanner and Justice got to the pond… But she couldn't allow herself to think of that. She'd go after them, find them along the road. How fast could a donkey carry two little boys?

"I'll take the horse," Luke said, walking quickly beside her. "I can go cross-country through the farm lanes and the woods. It will cut off nearly a mile."

"You can't expect me to stay here," Honor insisted.

"I'll take you in my buggy," Freeman volunteered. "Your little ones will be safe with my mother." He looked at Luke, who was already on the move. "There's a life ring with a rope on the pole by the spillway. You won't need it, but just in case."

Honor stifled a breathless moan. The image of her boys walking out on thin ice sickened her.

Luke stopped and turned to Honor. "Go back to the house and get your gloves. No sense in you catching your death if Justice and Tanner are playing somewhere along the road. I'm going to go right now but Freeman will bring around his buggy."

"God grant they are safe," she murmured.

She rushed to gather her mittens and tell Ivy where she was going, then came back out. By the time she walked down the porch steps, Freeman was bringing his horse and buggy to the back door. "Luke?" she asked. "Has he—"

"Already gone." Freeman offered his gloved hand to help her into the buggy. "He slapped a bridle on your horse and took off at a canter across the back field. Don't worry. If they did have any notion of going to play on the ice, he'll get there well ahead of them."

Honor's horse was a good one and had obviously been ridden before. Some driving horses balked or shied at a rider, but not this one. Luke hadn't seen a saddle in the barn, but he'd ridden bareback a lot in Kansas. His uncle's fields were vast compared to these farms, and what the elders didn't see, they couldn't object to. There was no gate at the edge of Honor's land but he'd brought wire cutters and he made short work of the three strands of barbed wire. No time to repair it today; that could wait. If the boys were headed for Freeman's pond, he needed to beat them there.

When the fence was down, he remounted, crossed another meadow and followed a lumber road through the woods. He knew the way; he'd walked this track once from the mill. He kicked the horse into a trot and then to a gallop. Beneath the trees, the ground was barely thawed and frost tinted the dry leaves. Ahead of him, a deer sprang up and vanished as soundlessly as a shadow. Luke urged his mount on.

Honor's sons knew that the pond, any pond, was strictly forbidden without an adult. Winter or summer. And they knew that leaving the property without telling their mother wasn't allowed. He couldn't help thinking that this is what came of being so lenient with them. Honor had allowed her children to grow willful and disregard her wishes. His own mother had been quick with a switch if he got out of line. That wasn't his way. He didn't believe in striking a child, in using any sort of physical punishment on any person, young or old. But there were other ways to discipline.

He left the field to ride along the edge of a farmyard and then reined the horse to a trot down their driveway to a paved road, the same route that led to the mill. The final quarter mile passed quickly with no sign of the boys. There was a grassy shoulder and Luke kept the animal on it at a steady lope.

"Let there be no one there," he muttered. "Please, let them have turned back."

A car pulled from the parking lot of the mill onto the blacktop and came slowly toward him. When the driver reached him, he came to a stop and rolled down his window. "Hey! There are two Amish kids out on the ice! I hollered to them but they wouldn't listen. I didn't know what else to do. Didn't seem to be any adults, so I called 911."

"Thank you!" Luke kicked the horse in the sides and galloped toward the edge of the pond. As he approached, he frantically scanned the ice for the children. A loud *eee-haw* came from the picnic area, and the horse whinnied as it caught the scent of its barn mate. Luke spotted the donkey tied to a picnic table just inside the trees. A small black Amish boy's hat lay on the bank. Frantically, Luke scanned the surface of the pond, catching sight of the two small figures about thirty yards from the shore. Tanner was tugging on a rope that held the partially submerged sled.

Luke vaulted from the horse's back. "Tanner!" he yelled, cupping his hands around his mouth. "Justice!"

One of them let out a wail.

"I'm coming! Lay down on your bellies!" he shouted in *Deitsch*. "Stretch out your arms."

Where were the rope and the flotation device Freeman had mentioned? He saw it and spent precious seconds to run to it and pull it free from the stake. Looping the rope over his shoulder, he eased out onto the ice. It crunched ominously, and a long crack zigzagged out to his left. Luke took another step and the ice gave under his weight. The heel of his boot sank through the surface. "God help me," he whispered. "Not by my doing, but by Yours."

Tanner flipped the sled over and then shrieked as one knee sank through the ice. Water welled up around him. Justice didn't make a sound. He lay flat, motionless, his face white under his black knit cap. About fifteen feet separated the two children.

Cautiously, Luke lowered himself to his hands and knees. "Tanner," he called. "Lay it on its back." The sled was a concave plastic disk rather than a traditional wooden sled; it might hold Tanner's weight if he fell through the ice.

Luke heard Justice whimper, but the boys were otherwise silent. Too afraid to speak, he imagined.

Luke inched forward, ignoring the groaning and snapping beneath him. One hand punched through and black water bubbled up. Far in the distance, he heard the wail of rescue vehicles. Luke kept moving, no longer on hands and knees but flat on his stomach, trying to push and pull himself across the ice.

Justice seemed secure for the moment, but Tanner was clearly in trouble. More cracks opened in the ice, and the child's knees crashed through the shimmering surface. Tanner managed to flip the sled over.

"That's it!" Luke shouted. "Hold on to it! It should float!"

Justice was quietly sobbing. His eyes were huge and frightened.

"Stay calm!" Luke urged. "Justice, I'm going to slide this life ring to you. Grab it and don't let go! Do you understand, Justice? Whatever happens, don't let go!"

On his first try, the ring missed the boy by six feet. Luke pulled it back and tried again. This time, it came within a yard of Justice. "Creep to the ring!" Luke ordered. "Slowly! There! You've got it! Now, don't move. Do you hear me? Do not move. I'll get you in a second."

He turned back to Tanner. Tanner was glued to the sled, cold water surging around his waist. Luke knew that time was against them. The water temperature could kill the children almost as quickly as drowning. He glanced at Justice. "Start crawling toward the shore," he called. Justice was the lightest of them. He might just make it to shore without falling through. "Whatever you do, Justice, don't let go of the ring!"

The shrieks of the emergency vehicles became louder, but Luke was afraid that if Tanner went through the ice, they wouldn't get there in time. "Keep moving!" he ordered Justice. Then he turned back to the older boy, "Hold on, Tanner, I'm coming to—"

The ice cracked and parted, and Luke felt himself

fall. Heard the splash. Water closed over his head, colder than anything he could imagine. His coat and boots filled with water and pulled him down, but he fought his way to the surface. His head broke the surface and he gasped for air. Both boys were screaming.

Tanner had gone down into the water, but the sled was holding him up. Luke attempted to crawl back up onto the ice, but every time he moved forward, it shattered and he sank again. He went under again and came up. This time his fingers touched the edge of Tanner's sled.

The boy had suddenly stopped screaming and was staring at him. Tanner held out a hand and Luke grasped it. He looked around, saw what he thought was a thicker section of ice, and shoved the sled as hard as he could. The sled glided up and over the ice, taking Tanner with it.

Luke's teeth were chattering so hard that he couldn't think. He was cold, so cold, and his boots were so heavy. Slowly, he used one foot to push off the right boot and then repeated the process with the left. His coat was next, but the zipper was almost more than he could manage.

He heard voices. On a bullhorn. The *Englisher* firemen were there, but he couldn't make out what they were trying to tell him. "Hold on," he tried to say to Tanner, but the words were as frozen as the chunks of ice around him. *Into Your hands*, he prayed silently. *In Your infinite mercy, spare these innocents...*

Luke kicked in the water, but he could feel himself sinking. He was suddenly tired, so tired. And then, the blackness closed over him and he didn't feel the cold anymore.

Chapter Thirteen

Luke sat up and looked around the cubicle in the hospital emergency room. "No," he repeated firmly to the nurse in scrubs adorned with multicolored cartoon characters. "I'm fine. I want to go home." He hated hospitals. He hated the smells and the sounds of sick people, and he could imagine how much money every minute he remained was costing him. The Amish didn't believe in medical insurance; the bill would be paid out of his own pocket. He'd certainly not have permitted anyone to take him to the hospital in an ambulance if he'd had his wits about him.

Although it was all pretty hazy in his mind, Luke knew that the fire company volunteers had reached him in time to keep him from drowning or dying from hypothermia. How they'd gotten to him, he wasn't so clear about. He'd coughed up a lot of water, and at one point he remembered an oxygen mask over his face, but he was all right now. He just wanted to get out of here.

The middle-aged nurse shook her head and spoke louder and more distinctly, almost as one would to a slow child. "The doctor would prefer that you remained with us for a few hours, Mr. Weaver, for observation."

Luke looked down, embarrassed to see that he was clad only in a scanty cotton hospital gown. Quickly, he pulled the thin, white blanket up to his neck. "Where are my clothes?"

She shook her head again. "I'm sorry, but the paramedics had to cut your things off when they treated you in the ambulance." She smiled.

"But the children are safe? Right? You said the children were fine."

She nodded. "Absolutely. I was told that the younger of the two didn't even need medical attention. The older boy is here with his mother, but they are just waiting for his paperwork. Apparently, he was more frightened than injured."

Luke closed his eyes for a moment. He remembered repeatedly asking the fireman about Tanner and Justice, but he'd been confused during the ambulance ride. He was relieved that the boys were okay and he said a quick, silent prayer of gratitude.

The nurse patted his hand. "Thanks to you, they were saved. That was very brave of you to go to their rescue. You nearly lost your own life in the effort. You're quite the hero, Mr. Weaver."

"Luke," he corrected. "My name is Luke, and I'm not a hero. Their lives were in God's hands. It is the Lord who deserves credit, not me."

"But a blessing that you came by when you did." She fluffed up his pillow. "Now, if you're feeling up to it, you have people waiting to see you."

"*Ya.* I mean, yes. And I want to see the doctor. I'm leaving as soon as I can get something decent to wear."

"I'll speak to him as soon as I can. One of our docs is out today, and we're all hard-pressed to care for everyone." She pushed a tall pole with tubes and a clear plastic bag hanging from it back away from his bed. "There's a gentleman in the waiting room, a Mr. Freeman. Perhaps he can help with your clothing. I am sorry that your things were ruined, but the hospital isn't responsible."

"No, I didn't think they were. Could you please send Freeman in?" He didn't bother to explain that Freeman was the miller's first name, not his last.

"I'll be glad to," she replied. She produced another blanket and laid it on the end of his bed. "You just lie back and rest. If you aren't warm enough, here's a second blanket."

"Warm enough, thank you."

The nurse gave him a final reassuring smile. "Don't be surprised if you make the front page of the *State News*," she said. "And the *News Journal*. There's a news crew parked outside. Everyone will want to know how you saved those children." As she left, she pulled the curtain closed, shutting off his cubicle from the rest of the emergency room.

Great, more newspapers, Luke thought. Just what he wasn't hoping to hear.

He didn't have long to wait before a grinning Freeman pushed his way through the curtains. "You know how to have a good time," he said. "Isn't it a little early to be swimming?" He was carrying a white trash bag and a man's straw hat in one hand. "Seems you have a problem hanging on to hats," he said, handing over the hat. "It isn't spring, but this was the best I could do.

My uncle offered one of his wool ones, but I think his head's smaller than yours."

"This will do fine," Luke answered. He smoothed back his hair and settled the hat on his head. "And you've got clothes for me in there, I hope."

"I do." Freeman grinned. "I got there in time to see one of the fireman cutting your trousers and shirt off. I brought shoes and socks, too. I don't know what happened to your boots."

Luke shrugged. "Bottom of the pond."

Freeman grimaced. "A worthwhile price, I'd say. Are they going to release you soon? I think Tanner is about ready to go home. I promised Honor I'd see them safely to the house. If you can go home with us, great. If not, I'll come back for you."

"I'll be ready to go as soon as I get dressed." Luke closed his eyes, then opened them. "But the boys are okay?" The memory of seeing Tanner break through the ice wouldn't leave him.

"Boys are fine."

"And the animals? I think I let the horse loose when—"

"Horse and mule are in my paddock. I'll have someone take them back to Honor's first thing in the morning. She came in the ambulance with you and Tanner. I called a driver. Plenty of room for you to go home with us." He held out his hand and Luke gripped it hard. "You did good," Freeman said. "If she'd lost one or both of those boys…"

"God preserved them," Luke said sincerely. "And you did the most by having that life ring and rope handy. Without it, I don't know what I would have done."

"Still, I'm pleased to call you my friend." Freeman

settled his hat further down on his head. "My mother was the one who came up with the idea for that ring. Insisted I buy it. It's been hanging there for three or four years and we never needed it."

"Not until today," Luke said. "I'd like to put these clothes on, and then we go."

"You go ahead. I'll go tell Honor you're going home with us. She wants to see you. She was just waiting until… She wanted to make certain that you were decent. No sense causing more trouble with the elders than we need to. They're already a little nervous over the Mystery Cowboy stuff from that newspaper in Pennsylvania. The bus accident. Not many of our people getting their pictures on the English television."

"Right. It wasn't by choice, I can tell you that." Luke glanced up at the clock on the wall. "Give me five minutes to get dressed, and then she can come in. I told the nurse that I wanted to leave. If they don't get back soon with my release papers, I'm going, anyway."

He had his garments on in two minutes. His chest burned, and his throat was sore. He had a little headache and water in one ear, but other than that, he didn't feel terrible, certainly not like a man who'd gone swimming in February. The pants and shirt had to be Freeman's, he judged. The shirt was a good fit, but the pants were long. Quickly, he adjusted the suspenders and slipped into the socks and shoes. He was just tying the last one when someone cleared her throat in the hall outside the curtain.

"Luke? Can I come in?"

It was Honor, and honestly, at that moment, he wasn't certain if he wanted to see her yet. Now that he was on his feet, he felt a little disoriented. And tired. So tired he could have lain down on the hospital bed and taken a nap. He took a deep breath, coughed and called, "*Ya*. Come in."

She stepped through the curtain and threw her arms around him, nearly knocking him back onto the bed. "Luke!" Her face was pale, her eyes red and swollen as if she'd been weeping, worry lines crinkling her flawless complexion. "I was so frightened," she said, switching from English to *Deitsch*.

Awkwardly, he hugged her back. He knew that this wasn't the time or place, but he was angry, and he couldn't hide it. Gently, he pushed her away. "Not here," he said. "We don't want the *Englishers* talking about our behavior."

"I don't care what they think. I love you. I have every right to hug you. Especially after what you did. You saved my babies. You—"

"They shouldn't have been there," he said. His voice came out gruff and rasping. "They had no business at the pond alone. Or on the ice at all."

"*Ne*, I know that." She swallowed, looking small and vulnerable beneath her bonnet, tugging at his heart.

But he would have his say. He couldn't let this be, couldn't hide his feelings. He'd done it long enough. He loved her and loving someone meant being honest with her. He truly believed that. "They could have died, Honor," he said. "Both of them. We could have lost them today."

Swirls of hurt glistened in her big brown eyes. Tears gathered and threatened to fall. "You think I don't know that? It was a terrible accident—could have been a terrible accident. But, by the grace of God and your courage and quick thinking, you saved them. You rescued my babies."

"*Ne*, Honor. It wasn't an accident."

"What do you mean?" She blinked, and the tears fell.

He felt as if a fist had stuck him full in the stomach, but he would do her no favors by holding back. "It wasn't an accident," he repeated. "It was carelessness."

"You're saying it's my fault? That I was careless with my sons?"

"You've let them run wild, Honor. You have allowed them to think they could do as they pleased, without consequences for disobedience. And your soft heart has nearly brought them and your family to ruin."

Her lower lip quivered, but she stiffened. "I thought it was *our* family. How can you say such a thing? I told them that they were never to go near a pond without an adult. They're children. They disobey sometimes. It's what children do." She wiped at her eyes with the back of her hands, trying to stop the tears. "That's a cruel thing to say, Luke. To blame me."

She began to sob, and his resolve crumbled.

He took her in his arms. "I'm sorry. I shouldn't have said that, at least not here. Not today. I know how you love them." She was weeping against his chest. "Shh, shh," he soothed. "I'm an idiot. I was so scared. I didn't think I could get to them in time. I'm sorry. But I've remained silent too often these last months, when I should have spoken. This is a serious matter, Honor, one we must settle before we marry."

She sniffed and looked up at him. "What do you mean?"

"You've made it clear that you don't want me to discipline the children. How do you expect me to be a father to them if I have no authority?"

"They are my children. It is my place to make them mind me."

"*Ne*, Honor, it can't be that way. When we marry, they'll be my children, as if born of my flesh. Either I'll be a father and a husband to you and your family, or this will never work between us."

"So, are you telling me that you've having second thoughts? You're talking about backing out of our wedding again?"

"Where would you get that idea?" He crushed her against him. "I'm never letting you go. You and the children are a package. I want to be your husband and their father, but this is something we have to face. Something must be done about their willfulness. We've got to set rules and there must be consequences for disobedience, even for the small ones. That's how you keep children from breaking the more serious rules."

"You're right." She glanced up at him. "They do get into trouble. And I am too softhearted to punish them as I should. But…if you'd… If you'll help me…" She started to cry again.

He looked around the small enclosure, saw a tiny box of tissues and retrieved them. He gave a handful to Honor and she blew her nose. "I'm sorry. I didn't mean to make you cry," he said.

"I know that you're right. I've worried about the same thing. It's just that Silas was so… He could be so stern with them. Once, he threatened Tanner with a belt."

"Did he beat him?"

She shook her head. "He tried to. I wouldn't let him.

I told him that if he laid a hand on Tanner in anger, I would take the children and leave him. He was so angry with me. He didn't speak to me for two days. He never did strike them, but he sent them to bed without supper and spoke to them so harshly when they misbehaved. I suppose, I think, I just tried to make up for his behavior by being too easy with them."

Luke hugged her again, just for a brief second. "We have to sit down and decide how we will handle misbehavior," he said quietly. "There should be small punishments for the small disobediences and larger ones for the more serious. What's important, I think, is that we both always react the same way. We act as a team, and then the children will know where we stand. And that they can't run from one to the other and expect to get away with mischief." He kissed the top of her forehead. "One thing I can promise you is that I will never raise a hand to our children. My father never did, either. He would talk to me quietly and make me understand what I had done wrong and why. His words pushed me to never make the same mistake again."

"I think that's a good plan," she said and reached for some more tissues. "I've let them get away with bad behavior, and I promise to try to do better." She took a step back. "I'd best get back to Tanner. Freeman is with him, but—"

Abruptly, the curtain pulled back and Luke heard the whirl of a digital camera. "There he is!" a young blonde woman in high heels and a tweed jacket exclaimed. "It's him! The cowboy hero. What do you do? Just ride around the country, looking for drowning people to rescue?" She stepped aside and a red-haired man with a camera on his shoulder moved forward to begin filming.

"No pictures," Luke said. He snatched off the hat Freeman had brought him and used it to cover his and Honor's faces. "We don't believe in having our image captured. Go away, please."

"Who is this woman?" the blonde demanded. "Is she the mother of the children? Can you tell us their names and ages?"

"We're saying nothing." Luke stepped in front of Honor, turning his back to the camera, still shielding their faces with the hat. "We are private people."

"Just a few questions," the persistent woman reporter insisted. "How does it feel to be a hero?"

The nurse with the silly cartoon scrubs swept in. "How did you get in here?" she said to the reporter and her companion. "Leave. Now, or I'll call security and…"

But Luke didn't hear the rest of her comment. He'd taken Honor by the arm and used the distraction to make his escape. The two of them slipped past the nurse and the newspaper people, and hurried down the hallway. He heard the sound of Tanner's voice and quickly located the curtain cubicle it was coming from. They stepped inside and he pulled the curtain shut behind them. Freeman sat on the side of the bed, showing Tanner a small, wooden marble game. If you placed a marble at the top of the tower, it would roll down, flipping switches. Tanner, red cheeked and hale, was laughing so hard that tears were running down his cheeks.

Tanner looked up when the two of them entered the room. Luke put his finger to his lips, and they all waited in silence while the nurse escorted the newspeople out of the emergency room, still fussing with them.

"Ready to go home?" Luke asked Tanner.

The boy nodded.

"Me, too," Luke said.

"And me." Honor reached over and squeezed Luke's hand. "Together."

He nodded. "Together."

Chapter Fourteen

"Take your time. Look around, and if you have any questions, I'll find the answers. My husband and his uncle aren't here today." Ruth Lapp waved toward the display area. "I don't usually help out at the chair shop because the children keep me busy at home, but our office girl had a dental appointment this afternoon. Fortunately, my sister Miriam offered to take my older children, so we didn't have to close."

She smiled down at the sleeping infant she wore in a baby sling made from dark green denim fabric. "This one seems to like being at the shop. He's been sleeping like a lamb most of the afternoon. Maybe he'll choose to be a woodworker like his father."

"Danke," Honor said.

Ruth was Hannah's oldest daughter. Her husband, Eli, and his uncle Roman, along with several other Amish craftsmen, designed and built most of the furniture for sale here. Honor didn't know Ruth as well as she did Rebecca or Leah, because Ruth was a little older, but she possessed the same vivid blue eyes and seemed as pleasant and helpful as her sisters.

Luke smiled. "A good choice for a man, if he does. Our Lord was a carpenter."

The phone rang in the small office, and Ruth excused herself. "Just come and find me if you see something you like."

Honor glanced at the clock on the wall behind the counter. "I hope the boys are behaving themselves." They'd been good since they'd gotten in so much trouble over going out on the ice, but she wasn't confident that they'd really reformed. "I'd hate to think that they were unruly for Katie. Maybe I should have brought one or two of them with us."

"Nope. Today is just for us," Luke said. "We need to pick out new bedroom furniture, and I promised you supper that you didn't have to cook."

"But the children… They can be a handful."

He smiled and shook his head. "You worry too much. Ivy and Katie are there to help Greta. I doubt much gets past Ivy. She's had experience with children for a lot of years. And Katie promised to bake ginger-boy cookies with them. They'll love that."

Honor grimaced, imagining her kitchen strewed with flour and dripping with molasses. "That's what I'm afraid of." But she smiled with him. Maybe she *was* being a worrywart. "It's sweet of you to want to take me to supper," she said. "But we don't have to go out to eat. You're going to enough expense, buying new furniture." She hesitated and then said what she was thinking. "You know, I'm not even sure we need to be here. There's nothing wrong with the bed and dressers I have now."

"Nothing wrong other than that Silas bought them for you." Luke glanced around to make certain that they were alone and then took her hand in his. "When we marry, I'll be moving into Silas's house, eating off his table—"

"*Ne*, that's my grandmother's table. She left it to me. The tall maple dresser in my bedroom was hers, too. You haven't seen that, but it's lovely. I'd hate to part with it."

"Let me finish," he said gently. "I don't really care where the table came from. It's a nice table. But, Honor…" He hesitated a moment and then went on. "The truth is that a man doesn't like the idea of another man's bed. I'm buying us a new one. After we're married, you can move the old one into one of the children's rooms, sell it or give it away. And you can certainly keep your grandmother's maple dresser for your clothes, but we need our own bed. Can you understand that?"

"*Ya.*" She nodded, liking the feel of his hand holding hers. But they weren't *Englishers*. Hand-holding in public wasn't something they did. She slipped her fingers out of his. "It's just the cost I was thinking of."

"Don't worry about the cost. I told you, I have substantial savings, and I also have the inheritance my uncle left me. This is what I've been saving my money for all these years. For you, Honor. For us."

She met his gaze and was so touched that she feared she might tear up. She loved that Luke felt so strongly that they belonged together. That he was so sure about this marriage. It helped her work through her own doubts.

Luke walked over to examine a queen-size oak bedstead. "What do you think of this style?"

"Umm, nice," she said noncommittally. She had to

admit that the thought of new furniture was a little bit exciting, but it was troublesome, as well.

Silas had always taken care that she knew how carefully he watched his money. He'd said she was too young to realize the value of it, especially since he was the one earning the income.

Only once could she remember arguing with him over money. She'd bought a cookie jar at Byler's, a silly thing shaped like a fat hen. The children had seen it and loved it, and since the holidays were approaching, she'd used part of her grocery allowance to buy it. Silas had made her return it, saying that it was an irresponsible purchase. But had it been an irresponsible purchase? She didn't think so. The cookie jar had made her laugh. And it had made her children happy. Couldn't money be used sometimes to bring happiness to the ones you loved?

Once she married, she would spend the rest of her married life obeying another man's wishes. At least now, if she wanted to make a foolish purchase with her own money, she could. Luke didn't seem to be miserly with his money, but what if she was misreading him?

Suddenly, marriage to Luke was a reality. It had all happened so fast. She loved him, certainly, but...she hoped she wouldn't live to regret her decision.

A woman should be married. Everyone said so; the church said so. It was the natural order of things. And doubly so for a woman with children. The incident on the ice had proved that, hadn't it? She couldn't care for her children properly alone. Her judgment wasn't always the best.

"Honor?"

"Ya?" She glanced up at him and realized that he'd

walked a few yards away to inspect a heavier bed with pineapples carved on the top of the posts. It was pretty, but probably more expensive than the first, plainer one. "Sorry, I was thinking about something."

"I can see that." He smiled at her. "Have you thought about what I asked you earlier? About going away for a honeymoon?"

"I don't know, Luke."

"We could go wherever you like," he said. "Maybe out West or to Florida. I've never seen palm trees, and it's a lot warmer there. We could go in the ocean."

It all sounded like a wonderful idea, but she knew he wouldn't want to take four children on his honeymoon, and she certainly couldn't leave them. She'd worry herself sick about them. And what would they think? That she'd abandoned them? It would be difficult enough for them to get used to having a new father, someone they would have to obey, without upsetting their daily routine by her taking a trip. "I don't think that would be a good idea. Not right away." She hedged. "I think it's best if we all stay at home and get settled in."

Luke ran his hand over the carving on the bedpost. "Most couples do go away for a few days after their marriage."

She pretended to look at the matching dresser. "Most couples don't already have four children. You didn't expect to take them with us, did you?"

"On our honeymoon?" He chuckled. "Definitely not. What I was hoping for was time alone with you."

"If you take me, you have to accept them, as well."

"Isn't that what I've been saying all along?" He moved closer and took her hand again. "Honor, it doesn't make me a bad father because I want to be alone for a few days with my bride. But if you think it isn't a good idea, I'll accept that. For now. But later, maybe in the summer, once I have the crops in the ground, we'll go somewhere, just the two of us. I'll hire a driver. We could go to Niagara Falls or even out to Kansas. Lots of people have been volunteering to watch our kids, and you know Katie and Freeman would take good care of them."

"I know they would, but…" She sighed. She didn't know what was wrong with her. The last three months with Luke had been the happiest, best weeks of her life. Why couldn't she just accept God's gift of Luke, and the happiness he brought her and her children, and enjoy it? Why was she second-guessing herself? "It's not something we have to decide today, is it?"

She was feeling a little overwhelmed. It seemed there were so many decisions to make all at once. Luke had insisted on taking her out today and choosing furniture when she had so much to do at home. Her wedding clothes were cut out and waiting to be stitched up. And Sara wanted her to come by and help her decide what they would serve for the wedding supper.

Aunt Martha had wanted to visit this afternoon, and Honor had had to tell her that she wouldn't be home because she and Luke were going to town. In a way, Honor was glad to have an excuse. Aunt Martha had let everyone in the county know that she thought Honor was rushing into a marriage with a less-than-suitable man, and Honor was sure that she was only coming to try to get her to change her mind. Martha had been one of her mother's best friends, and Honor respected her for that. She didn't want to be rude, but the older woman was wrong about Luke. He was a good man, and Honor loved him. She was going to marry him, and that was that. But having Aunt Martha to deal with when she was already at her wit's end only added icing to the cake.

"So, which set do you like best?" Luke asked, walking away to stand back and have another look at the furniture. "There's the oak one over there, but I'm not crazy about the low dresser with the mirror."

She sighed. "I don't know. Whichever one you want," Honor said.

He shook his head. "*Ne*, love. It's for you to choose. I want to make you happy."

That made her smile. "I know that, I just…" She didn't finish her sentence because she didn't know how to articulate what she was feeling. It was almost as if she was afraid this was all too good to be true.

He stood there, looking at her for a moment. "It is a little scary, isn't it? The wedding?" he said, almost seeming to know what she was thinking. "Making such big changes in our lives. But Freeman says everybody feels the same way." He folded his arms across his chest. "Now, please pick out a bedroom set for us, unless you don't like any of them." He shrugged. "And then we can go somewhere else. I just thought we'd get the best quality coming here."

"No, no, these pieces are beautiful and sturdy and… I like the one with the pineapples," she admitted.

"Me, too. That's my favorite. Will there be room for the tall dresser if we keep the one you already have?"

"*Ya.*" She nodded. "It's a big room."

"*Goot.* So, we'll take the bed, the side tables and the dresser, and I'll make arrangements to have them delivered out to the farm." He pointed in the direction of the office where Ruth had gone. "Let me pay for them, and then we'll have our driver take us to the mall."

"I thought we were going to supper."

"We are, but first, we need to go somewhere to buy sheets, blankets, towels, that kind of stuff."

She smiled at him as she traced the lines of the pineapple on a foot post with her index finger. "Are you sure? This is going to be a very expensive day."

"You're worth it," he assured her.

"I hope so," she replied, looking up at him. "Because once we're married, it will be for keeps."

The waitress, a teenager with a brown ponytail, brought their orders and put them on the table. "Be careful," she warned cheerfully. "Everything's hot." She balanced her tray expertly on one hip and removed two glasses of iced tea. "Anything else I can get you?"

"No, thank you," Luke said.

Honor looked down at her supper. It smelled delicious. The special tonight at Hall's restaurant was meat loaf and boiled potatoes. She'd chosen collards and green beans to go with it. This had turned out to be a wonderful afternoon. After she'd gotten over her nervousness at picking out the furniture, she and Luke had walked around the mall and bought crisp white sheets and a beautiful blue comforter for their bed, as well as some new towels.

This was really happening.

She was marrying Luke, and nothing would be like it had been in her first marriage. The shopping trip was proof of that. The first time that she was married, the only new things they got for their house were gifts given to her. Everything else was a hand-me-down.

Not that there was anything wrong with perfectly good used household items, but a young girl just settling into her first house with her new husband takes great pride in her housewifery skills, and a set of new dish towels or a fresh broom can go a long way to making a house a home.

"Grace?" Luke said quietly and surprised her by reaching across the small table and taking her hands in his.

She inhaled sharply and glanced around to see if people were looking at them. But the other diners were all busy with their own conversations. No one was staring at them. Their driver, Jerry, was seated at a booth near the side door with his wife, Jan, and there was even another Amish couple at another table. Hall's was a neighborhood restaurant in a small town where locals came for traditional food and friendly service. She could feel at ease here, even if most of the people were *Englishers*.

Honor bowed her head for silent prayer. She knew that her thoughts should be on giving thanks to God for all His blessings, and especially for this meal, but it was difficult to focus when she was so conscious of Luke's touch and the tingling that ran up her arms.

When he opened his eyes, he looked directly into hers and smiled. "It's been a good day, hasn't it?"

"It has," she answered truthfully. Excitement bubbled through her and she found that she was starving. She brought a forkful of the meat loaf to her lips and tasted it. "Mmm. Just as good as I remembered. I'd like to have the recipe, but the cook won't give it out."

"Maybe I should bring you here every week," Luke teased.

She chuckled. "Not every week, but now and then. They don't have meat loaf all the time, but they do make a good liver and onions."

He made a face. "Not on my list of favorites."

"*Ne?* And I was planning on cooking it every Monday evening." She chuckled at his expression. "Just teasing. The children don't like it, either."

"Then I'm saved." He smiled at her as he buttered his roll. "Are you happy with the furniture we picked out?"

"I am. I'm glad we liked the same set." She couldn't stop looking at him. He was so solid, so handsome, so full of life that it was almost too good to be true that he wanted to be her husband and the father of her children.

In many ways, this was the Luke she'd loved as a girl, but there was something more about him. He was stronger, steadier, and seemed to glow with an inner enthusiasm whether he was opening a hymnal or tackling a tough task in the field. How foolish she'd been to resist his courting. This was truly the man God had planned for her.

"At least we agree on something," Luke said. She must have looked confused, because he quickly added, "The bedroom suite. We both like pineapples." He chuckled, and they laughed together.

She tasted the collards. They were tender and seasoned perfectly. "It was nice of you to buy the new things at the mall," she told him. "My sheets were getting shabby."

"After we're married, we'll open a joint bank account with my savings," Luke said. "You can write a check for anything you need for yourself or for our household. And whatever Silas left you is yours, for your children or for your security. I don't want any of it."

"That's kind of you," she replied.

"Not kind," he said. "Fair. You should have security, in case I should die or become..."

She put down her fork. "Don't say such a thing."

"It's possible. Farming accidents happen. Illnesses happen, Honor. I want to be certain that you will be cared for, no matter what comes."

She shook her head. "For that, we must trust in God." She smiled at him. "But this was supposed to be our night out. Can't you think of anything more pleasant to talk about than you dying?"

He reached out and patted her hand. "We can talk about anything you'd like, or we can just sit here and eat and I can look at you."

"Don't say such things," she whispered, feeling her cheeks grow warm. But secretly it pleased her. It had been a long time since she'd felt pretty or that a man cared about what she wanted or what she thought. How easy it was to forget the years that she'd resented him and remember the good times they'd had together, the laughter and the fun.

Luke began to talk about the wedding, and she found that, despite her nervousness, she was looking forward to the day. She wished that her children could be part of the celebration, but by custom, the wedding would be just for adults. Friends would care for them until the following day. She hoped the kids would understand. The marriage ceremony was a serious ritual, and she needed to give all her attention to the words of the bishop and the preachers, and, of course, to Luke.

"You haven't met my cousin Raymond, but you'll like him and his wife. They're coming to the wedding because I want you to meet them. They have two children. The oldest is six, I believe. Anyway, work has been slow for Raymond in Kansas. He's thinking of moving his family here. He'd like to raise goats for meat and for milk. His wife makes the best cheese." Luke took a mouthful of potatoes and chewed slowly. "I was wondering if you might be interested in selling them that acreage on the far side of the road. I can't think that we'll ever need it, and you said you'd wondered if you should sell it. The fields are in good pasture, perfect for a dairy operation. What do you think?"

She looked up in surprise. "I don't know. Do you think they'd want to be so far from Dover and the other Amish communities?"

Luke leaned forward, his expression enthusiastic. "I don't because here's why. I was thinking that one way to fix the problem of being so far from your Amish community is to attract more young Amish families out to where we are. Raymond has an unmarried sister who's been teaching school for three years. If he moves, she'll come with him. Our children need a school nearby. Tanner really should have started first grade last fall."

The implied criticism stung a little. But she knew he was right. "Yes, Tanner should have gone," she said. "But the nearest Amish school is farther than he could walk alone, and getting all the children organized to drive him back and forth would have taken a lot of effort, especially in bad weather." She felt her cheeks and throat flush. "Besides, he'd just lost his father, and—"

"Not just, Honor," Luke corrected. "It's been more than a year since Silas died. It's time Tanner was in school like every other boy his age. It is the state law. You can't continue to coddle him."

"I'm not coddling him," she defended herself. "I intended to send him this coming September."

"Good. We agree on that, too. And that's why having Raymond's boy in the neighborhood would be an asset. We can start a school with two children. We just have to figure out where we want to build it. And when Tanner's a little older, he could walk, or we could buy him a pony to ride to school."

"I'm not letting a young child ride a horse on the road. The traffic…"

Luke chuckled. "He won't be seven for long. He'll be eight and then nine. He'll be responsible enough to be trusted with a horse. And you have to consider that the other boys will need schooling. Not to mention Anke."

"Anke's just a baby."

Luke shook his head. "Freeman and I have talked about this. He and Katie are planning to sell off several plots, to encourage Amish families to settle near the mill. I think they're even considering donating a little land to build a school. With them expecting."

Honor looked down at her plate. It was unusual of an Amish man to comment on a woman being in the family way, but she thought she liked it. Too many men pretended babies just fell from God's arms out of the sky.

"Your relatives have moved, either west or to Virginia, because land is so expensive here," Luke went on. "But your soil is rich. For a small specialty farm or for those who are craftsmen, they don't need a lot of acreage. And you don't have the bitter winters we had in Kansas."

Suddenly Honor was feeling a little overwhelmed. More decisions. She looked down at the napkin on her lap. "I'm still not sure that I should sell land. I have four children. Maybe I should save all of the farm for them."

"I don't want to put any pressure on you, Honor. But think of it. We could build a community like Seven Poplars. We're only two families now, but in five years…"

"I *will* think about it," she promised. "And I did know that Tanner had to go to school. I just didn't think that it would hurt him to start a little later. I needed his help with the younger boys."

But, as she said it, she realized how lame it sounded. Tanner really wasn't that much help around the farm. At least, he hadn't been until she and Luke had decided together that she needed to ask more of the children. It wasn't easy to suddenly let someone else advise her on what to do with her sons, but there was a relief in not having to do it all alone.

She gave Luke a small smile. "I've been doing things on my own since Silas died," she said. "I know everything will be different after we're married, and I also know that will be a good thing. But…" Her smile deepened. "You'll have to be patient with me, because this is all happening pretty fast."

"Not fast enough for me." He broke into a grin. "But then, I've been waiting for this wedding for a long time."

Chapter Fifteen

The day of their wedding dawned bright and sunny, with only the slightest breeze and more blooming daffodils and early tulips than Luke had ever seen surrounding one house. He'd arrived at Sara's at five thirty in the morning to find her already up and buzzing around the kitchen.

Two cups of her strong coffee later, he'd joined six couples in Sara's hospitality barn where chickens were being prepared for roasting and trays of creamed celery, stuffing, apple crisp and pies were being assembled, ready for the commercial ovens. And more helpers would be arriving for a wedding where they were expecting nearly a hundred guests.

Luke had wanted a simple wedding, but there was no arguing with Sara once she set her mind on something. Several of his cousins and his brother and family had come from the Midwest to share in the happiness of the day, but Honor had few relatives. Most of the guests would be friends and neighbors and the extended Yoder family, as well as several of Sara's clients. The awaited assurance of his baptism and standing in his home church had finally come through, and Honor's bishop had agreed to perform the ceremony. Three couples would be sharing the *Eck*, or wedding table, with them: Freeman and Katie; Rebecca and her husband, Caleb; and a longtime friend of Honor's, Mary Beth, and her husband, Moses, who had come from Kentucky.

Freeman helped Luke to set up chairs in the main room of the barn. The preaching service and the actual wedding ceremony would take place in the house, but the dinner and, later, the evening supper would be held here in the barn. This was a building that Sara had rescued and had remodeled for entertaining. As a professional matchmaker, Sara needed a place to bring couples together. The outside might look like a red barn, but inside the only similarity was the loft area. The downstairs space was spacious and as tidy as Sara's living room, and the commercial kitchen was more than adequate for serving large groups of guests.

At eight o'clock, Sara bustled into the barn and inspected the preparations. The *Eck* had been set up in one prominent corner. Other long tables filled much of the remaining space. By custom, and for practicality, the *Eck* hadn't been decorated with wedding flowers. Instead, there was a snowy white table covering, beautiful antique dishes and blue and white pottery pitchers, which would later be filled with cold water, lemonade and apple cider. There would be cakes, pies and candies, as well as bowls of apples and oranges. Sara made a few adjustments to napkins and place settings and pronounced the *Eck* perfect for the bride and groom.

"You'd better change into your good clothing," she said to Luke. "It's laid out for you in the men's bunkhouse." Sara chuckled. "Hannah sent over two new wool hats for you, since you seem to have such trouble holding on to yours."

Luke grimaced, but took the teasing with good humor. Though he and Honor had chosen to have the wedding here instead of at Hannah and Albert's home, Hannah had appointed herself his honorary mother. As part of their wedding gift, she'd sewn a complete set of clothing for him, including a black wool *mutze*, the formal coat wore by Amish men for church services and important events, matching trousers and a vest. The garments had taken hours and hours to complete, and Luke knew that, with care, they would last him for years.

As he walked to the small building where the matchmaker housed her visiting male clients, Luke could hardly contain his excitement. In just a short while, Honor would join him in an upstairs room of Sara's house, where they would meet with the elders of the church. There, one of the preachers would speak to them about the duties and responsibilities of marriage and be certain that each entered this union of their own free will. Below, the guests would begin the first hymn of the service. He and Honor would follow the elders and the bishop downstairs and would take their seats near the front of the room.

The sermon would be two to three hours in length, after which the bishop would invite him and Honor to come up and exchange their vows. Luke's heart beat faster and he thought of his promise to cherish and care for Honor, to respect her and remain with her for the rest of their lives. He would utter these words in front of God and all the witnesses, and she would repeat the same. A few more words from the bishop, and they would be married.

His chest felt tight; his throat clenched. So long he'd waited and prayed for this day. He was so happy that he might have been made of mist instead of flesh and blood, so light that he could have vaulted over the house in one leap.

Honor… His Honor. His family.

Almost feeling as if he was in a dream, he dressed, his fingers wooden as he fumbled to pull up his stockings and adjust his suspenders. The trousers, coat and vest fitted him perfectly. How Hannah had managed it, he couldn't guess. He'd never stood for a measuring. Honor had told him that she would be wearing blue. He loved her in blue. There would be no veil, no flowing train as the English women wore. Her new dress and apron, cape and *kapp* were exactly like those she wore to worship services, but after tonight, she would fold the garments carefully away to only be worn again on the day of her funeral.

He blinked, nudged out of his dreamy and pleasant thoughts by the prospect of Honor's death. God willing, that would be far-off, in His time, when they had grown old together. Hopefully, there would be more children, grandchildren and even great-grandchildren before their time on Earth was ended.

Today was no time to think of partings or of the eternal life in Heaven that awaited those who lived according to God's teachings. Today was about new beginnings, about taking up a life of promise and love, about being with Honor every day and every night. Together, they had promised each other. It was all he wanted. Together, they would make a home for their children and teach them the values that had been handed down through the generations by their faith.

"Luke!" After a quick knock on the door, Freeman opened it a crack. "Are you dressed? The preachers have arrived. You'd better move along. You don't want to keep the bishop waiting."

"Coming," Luke said, putting on the first hat he could lay hands on. That, too, fitted him as well as... He chuckled. As well as if it had been made for him. How had Hannah guessed the exact size of his head? "I guess mothers know these things," he murmured under his breath.

Luke joined Freeman outside on the sidewalk. "Is Honor here? Have you seen her?" He glanced around. Dozens of buggies were arriving. Teenage boys were taking charge of the horses. Clusters of guests were making their way into the house. Luke chuckled again. He'd thought he'd only been a few minutes in getting dressed. But he had been woolgathering. The time had flown. Excitement surged through him.

"Getting nervous?" Freeman asked. He strode shoulder to shoulder with him, a steady friend.

"Ne," Luke answered. *"Ya.* I suppose I am." He couldn't help thinking back to the last time they'd intended to marry. Had he felt this excited? He didn't think so. That seemed a lifetime ago, as though it had happened to another person. He'd been a boy then, too young and foolish to know what he wanted in life... too immature to realize what he was throwing away by walking out on her.

"There's the bishop." Freeman indicated the approaching buggy drawn by a gray mare. "You'd best get upstairs. Honor's probably up there waiting for you."

And scared out of her mind that I won't show, Luke thought.

He went in through the back door, crossed the kitchen full of women and walked up the stairs. He couldn't wait to see her…couldn't wait to see her face. To marry her as he hadn't been able to do that day years ago.

I'll make it up to her, he promised silently. *I'll never let her down again.*

The door to the designated chamber stood open. Rebecca waited just inside. But he didn't see Honor anywhere. There were the two preachers and the deacon. There was Freeman's uncle, a respected elder of the church. But there were no other women. He scanned the room twice before turning to Rebecca. "She's not here yet?" he asked her quietly.

Rebecca's concern showed on her lovely face. "Not yet," she confirmed. "But she'll be here any moment. Don't worry. Katie and Ivy are bringing her. It's quarter to nine. The service doesn't start for another fifteen minutes."

"It's just…it's not like Honor to be late," he said. Honor always wanted to be at church a half hour before the first hymn. She thought it disrespectful to come in last. He exhaled softly and edged to the window to look out. Was it possible something had happened to delay them? An accident or mishap with the buggy? The horse throwing a shoe?

The bishop entered the room and shook hands all around. "Bride not here yet?" he asked. Someone made a joke about women primping on their special day, and everyone laughed but Luke.

Luke removed his hat and placed it on a dresser beside other hats. Warm dampness rose at the back of his shirt collar and he rubbed absently at his neck. The minutes ticked away. He went to the window again and then looked at Freeman.

"I'll go down and check to see if she's arrived," his friend said. "I wouldn't think Katie would let the time get away from her. Not today."

One of the preachers began to tell about a longer-than-usual sermon he'd heard on a visit to an Amish community in western Virginia. It was an amusing tale, but the bishop laughed a little too loudly. Somewhere downstairs, a clock chimed.

"Nine o'clock," the deacon remarked. He said something quietly to the bishop and then nodded at Luke as he exited the room.

"My apologies," Luke said to the bishop. "I'm sure she'll be here any minute." He followed the deacon down the steps. As he left the house by the back way, the guests were rising for the first hymn. Luke walked into the yard, empty now of boys and horses. He glanced down the driveway. He could see the road. There were no buggies in sight.

Freeman came up beside him. "Don't get yourself into a fever," he said. "She'll be here. She's just late."

Luke turned to him, shoulders stiff and hands tingling. "Honor's not late," he said, voicing the unthinkable. "She's not coming."

One hour earlier...

"What do you mean you aren't going?" Katie called through Honor's closed bedroom door. "I know you're nervous, but there's no time to waste. We have to hurry, or we'll be late for service."

"Is she ready?" Ivy's voice came from down the hallway. "Do you know what time it is?" Honor heard her ask Katie. "The bishop and the elders will be waiting. Not to mention the wedding guests. And Luke, poor Luke will be pacing the floor."

"She says she's changed her mind," Katie answered. "She said she's not marrying Luke Weaver today or any day."

Honor blew her nose.

"Atch," Ivy remarked, outside the door now. "Wedding jitters."

Honor wiped her eyes. "Common sense," she whispered, too softly for either Ivy or Katie to hear.

There was a rapping on the door. "Honor. Will you let me come in and talk to you?" Ivy called.

"Ne! There's no need. I made a mistake and I have to right it now, while I still can. I thought I wanted to marry Luke, but I don't," Honor said. "Please go and tell the bishop that I've reconsidered my decision."

"Luke will be devastated," Katie said, sounding close to tears. "Please, won't you let us in so we can talk about it?"

"I'm sorry. I just can't do it," Honor replied.

She heard the two whispering, and then Katie called out, "You're sure you want us to go without you? You're certain about this? You don't just want to take a minute to catch your breath? Maybe spend a few minutes in prayer?"

"I'm certain I want you to go," Honor answered, fighting tears. "Tell everyone I'm sorry."

There was more whispering, and then Ivy said, "If you're sure that's what you want."

What she wanted? Honor didn't know what she wanted, but she replied, *"Ya,* go, please." She heard

Katie say something that she couldn't make out and then footsteps echoing down the steps. Minutes later she heard the rattle of buggy wheels. She went to the window to watch Katie and Ivy roll out of the yard.

Then Honor sank down on the bed and buried her face in her hands. What would she say to the children? How could she explain to Sara, who'd been so good to her? And how could she face Luke ever again?

But, for better or worse, her decision was made and she'd have to live with it. She should have felt relief, but instead, all she felt was sadness.

Luke tugged on the brim of his new hat. "Honor did this on purpose. She did it to get even for what I did to her," he said stoically. "She planned this all along."

"Ne." Sara shook her head. "I don't believe that, and neither do you. Not really. You're just smarting right now. Honor doesn't have a spiteful bone in her body."

Sara, Albert and Freeman had followed Luke out of the house and into the yard. They stood in the grass near the back porch. None of the wedding guests, except for Ivy and Katie, who had brought word, knew there was no bride.

"Here's my question to you. Do you love her?" Sara asked, looking Luke in the eyes. "If you could fix this, would you?"

He glanced away. Emotion brought moisture that clouded his eyes, and he was afraid that he'd make himself appear even more of a fool than he was. "It's too late," he answered gruffly.

"It may not be," Albert put in. "They're only on the second hymn. It will be a long sermon."

"I agree," Freeman said. "If you want to try to change

her mind, there's time." He glanced at Katie, who'd come to stand beside him. "Did you know that we almost broke up right before we married? I was to blame."

"*Ne*, Freeman," Katie said, taking his hand. "We were *both* to blame."

Freeman smiled down at her. "My Katie left me and I had to chase her down." He chuckled. "It was a lot farther than you'd have to go."

Luke scuffed the ground with one foot, sending up a small cloud of dust. He rubbed his hands together as he fought to compose himself. He'd been so happy, and now everything was lost. "It's because of the children," he admitted gruffly. "I thought she let them get away with too much, and I said so. I told her it wouldn't be that way after we were married."

"I don't think it's about that," Sara insisted. "I really think it's cold feet. Her last marriage was difficult. I expect she's afraid that she's climbing out of the frying pan and into the fire."

"You think she's afraid of me?" he asked, looking up at the matchmaker. "I'd never harm her. I'd never make decisions that weren't the best for her and for our children. I'll always put them first."

"So, convince her of that," Sara said.

"Go talk to her, Luke." Freeman laid a hand on his shoulder. "If Honor's worth having, she's worth trying to hold on to. Don't let pride stand in the way of fixing this."

Luke stood there in indecision. He wanted to go, but—

"Do you have a driver's license?" Albert asked.

"What?" Luke turned to him.

"Are you allowed to drive, legally?" Albert asked. "I thought you mentioned to me you knew how to drive."

"*Ya*, I have a driver's license. I needed one in Kansas to deliver my uncle's grain to the buyer." Luke frowned. "Why do you ask?"

The older man pointed to a small black SUV parked next to the barn. "Take Hannah's daughter Grace's car. The keys are in it."

"Take her car?" Luke asked, unsure of what he'd just heard.

"She's my daughter, too," Albert said. "And Grace would be the first to agree that this is an emergency. Go get your bride, Luke. Or you'll have to explain to Hannah why she made you that fine suit and baked all those pies for nothing."

Luke banged on the back door of the house. "Unlock the door, Honor!"

She stared at the door, glad the window was still covered with a board. Rather than fix the window, she and Luke had decided to replace the whole door and they were waiting for it to come in at the lumberyard.

"Honor!"

She took a shuddering breath. She hadn't believed that he would come for her. And when she'd heard the motor vehicle come up the driveway, she wondered who he'd gotten to drive him over from Sara's.

Honor's heart was pounding so hard that she thought it might fly out of her chest. How had she allowed this to go so far? What had made her agree to marry Luke in the first place? What had ever made her think it was a good idea?

"Be reasonable! We need to talk!"

"*Ne!* I don't want to talk to you!" Honor slid the bolt. "Go away!"

"No one is going to force you to marry me," Luke said. "I wouldn't do that. I just want to talk to you. I need to know why."

"It's for the best!"

He knocked louder. "You're angry about the children, about my trying to interfere with your parenting. I understand. I'm just trying to help. Because I love them, too. But we can talk about this, Honor. We can figure it out."

"I'm not talking to you. Go away!"

"I will not go away until we've talked face-to-face," he hollered. "I'm coming in!"

Then she heard nothing.

"Luke... Luke?" Had he given up? She ran to a window and tried to see if he was still on the back step, but it was out of her line of vision. What she did see was a stepladder moving in the direction of the kitchen window. "You wouldn't," she whispered. Then she heard the squeak of the ladder being opened.

Luke's hat and then his determined face appeared on the other side of the glass. "I'm coming in," he warned and began to push up the window.

Honor dashed from the laundry room, through the kitchen and up the stairs into her bedroom. She heard footsteps just before she slammed the door and threw the latch. "There," she declared, spinning around to stare at the paneled door. That would put an end to this nonsense. She didn't have to talk to him if she didn't want to. She'd decided what was best, and that was that.

Footsteps pounded up the staircase. "Honor?" Her doorknob turned. "Honor, please."

"I'm not letting you in. I can't marry you." Honor began to push one of the new bedside tables in front of the door.

"Honor, listen to me."

"*Ne*, go away, Luke." She shook her head again and again, feeling a sense of panic. "I'm sorry. I'm sorry."

"You are going to talk to me," he repeated. He banged on the door. "Just open it."

"I have nothing to say to you."

"Well, I have something to say to you. I love you," Luke called from the other side of the door. "I want to make you my wife. Why are you doing this?"

"Because I love you," she whispered, too low for him to hear her. "Because I don't want to ruin your life or my children's."

"What?" he shouted. "I can't understand what you're saying. Are you going to open the door and talk to me like an adult?"

She didn't answer. Couldn't answer. If she did, she'd start crying again, and she'd wept too many tears.

"Please open the door."

"*Ne.*"

She heard him walk away and her heart sank. Her knees went weak and she steadied herself against one of the beautiful pineapple bedposts of the bed he'd put together the previous day. For their new life together. He'd set up the whole room, but first he'd cleaned the whole place top to bottom, and it smelled of lemon wood polish.

She didn't deserve him. Luke needed a sensible wife, someone with good judgment, someone he could rely on. She knew that she'd hurt him, but in time he'd come to realize that she'd made the best decision.

She went to the window but didn't see him. The black automobile stood in the yard, and she wondered where the driver was. She looked at the mantel clock. Quarter to ten. The bishop would be preaching Honor's wedding sermon and she wasn't there to hear it. What would her friends think of her? Sara Yoder would be crushed by her rejection of the match. She knew that Katie and Ivy were disappointed in her. She'd failed them all.

The footsteps came back up the steps. "Last chance, Honor," Luke said. "Open the door, or I'm taking it off the hinges."

He can't do that, she thought. Hinges are on the inside, not the outside. But the bedrooms had had no doors when they moved into the farmhouse, and Silas had hung them all backward so that they opened out into the hall, not into the rooms. He'd made a mistake, one she'd wanted to tease him about, but hadn't dared. It was a mistake he'd promised to fix, but like so many of Silas's promises, he'd never kept it.

Metal scraped against metal and the top hinge squealed as Luke pulled out the pin. "One question," he called. "Answer one question for me."

She was shaking. "Will you leave if I do?"

"Maybe," he replied, as he pried at the bottom hinge. "What is it?"

"Can you tell me that you don't love me?"

"You'll go if I do… If I tell you that I don't love you?"

"I will. If you tell me to my face, not through a door."

She breathed a sigh of relief. God forgive her, all she had to do was to tell a tiny untruth. Just say the words, and he'd go away and leave her in peace. Simple. But it was the most difficult thing anyone had ever asked her to do. She opened her mouth and tried to speak. Nothing came out.

"Thought so," Luke answered. He removed the pin from the bottom hinge. "One to go."

She ran back to the second nightstand and began to push it toward the door, but she was too late. The door sagged and swayed, and then Luke lifted it and moved it aside. He shoved aside the first nightstand aside and walked into her bedroom.

"You can't come in here with me," she protested weakly. "It isn't decent."

"Ne," he agreed. "It isn't, but after tonight, it will be our bedroom."

"Why can't you understand?" she cried, bringing her hands to her cheeks. "Why can't I make you see that I can't marry you?"

Luke sat on the corner of the nightstand and folded his arms. He took off his hat and tossed it onto the top of the tall dresser that stood at an angle to the door. "Explain it to me."

She began to tremble harder. Her throat felt as if it was closing up and her stomach turned over. How fine he looked in his new clothing. She could see how angry he was. But she didn't feel afraid of him, as she had been with Silas. She knew Luke would never harm her.

"You love me, and I love you," he said quietly. "You promised to marry me, and now you say you don't want to. What have I done wrong, Honor?"

She shook her head. "Nothing," she said, hugging herself inside the knit wrap. "It's not you, it's me. I'm afraid. Terrified that if I marry you, I'll ruin everything for you and for my children."

He opened his arms.

She ran to him, finding solace when she laid her head against his chest. "Don't you see?" she sobbed. "I've made so many bad decisions. Over and over. I insisted you and I get married when we were too young. You wanted to wait, but I wouldn't. I told you that I wouldn't wait for you if we didn't marry then. And with the children... My boys almost drowned because I'm a terrible mother."

He cradled her against him. "You're not a bad mother, Honor. You're a wonderful mother. You're dedicated to your children. And you can't blame yourself for what happened between us nine years ago. We were both immature."

"But you left me the morning of our wedding."

"It wasn't you. It was always me," he said, burying his face in her hair. Her *kapp* fell back onto her neck, but neither of them noticed. "I left because I knew that you would never abandon your faith. And I didn't know if mine was strong enough...if I could live Amish. I couldn't ask you to leave with me."

She raised her head and looked into his eyes. "But you'd accepted baptism."

"That made it worse, that I doubted my faith after I'd given my pledge to remain true to our beliefs."

"But you didn't leave the church. And you believe now. Your faith is strong."

He nodded. "I do believe now. I grew up, Honor. God spoke to me, not to my ears, but in my heart. I knew that He was the right way, the only way. I wanted to come back for you, but by then, you'd already married someone else."

"That was another mistake I made," she told him. "Marrying Silas, staying with him once I knew what he was, letting him control our money, control me. If I was a good mother, I would never have let him be so hard with the children. I was supposed to protect them."

"And you did. You told me that you wouldn't let Silas strike them."

"But…but…"

"You're human. You make mistakes, just like I do. Once you were in the marriage, you stayed to try to make the best of it. But that shouldn't keep you from marrying me, from reaching for happiness, Honor." He tilted her face up with a big hand and tenderly kissed her lips. "Why didn't you come this morning…? Why wouldn't you talk to me?"

"Because I was afraid. Afraid that if I was making another mistake by marrying you, my children would suffer, you would suffer. If I messed up my first wedding and then did the same with the second, how could I be certain that the third would be any different?"

The barest smile appeared on his face as he looked down on her. "Do you love me, Honor?" he asked.

"You know that I do."

"Then join with me in marriage in the sight of God and our church. Today. Now."

She closed her eyes. Not knowing what to say, what to do. She knew what she wanted to do. "But what if…"

"Have faith, Honor. Faith in us, faith in the Lord God. That's all you need, a little faith. Because you won't have to make all these decisions alone anymore. We'll do it together. And if we make mistakes, which we will, we'll work to make them right again. Together. It's all any of us can do. Try, every day. Try to do the right thing and try to live as our beliefs teach us."

"But it's too late," she murmured, still holding on tightly to him. "I was supposed to be there at nine."

"It's never too late," Luke assured her. "I've got Grace's car. I can have us at Sara's house in fifteen minutes." He leaned back to look at her, still holding her in his arms. "Now, dry your eyes, straighten your *kapp*, and let's go. Because, unless I'm sadly mistaken, our bishop won't be halfway through his sermon."

"Do you think so?" she asked.

"I do. And if he's as hungry as I think he'll be when he reaches the end of his sermon, he'll still marry us so that he can sit down to that fine wedding dinner that Sara and Hannah have prepared."

She offered him a faint smile, wiping at her eyes as she took a step back from him. "We'll be a scandal. Showing up late to our own wedding. Together."

He met her gaze. Held it. "Enough to keep your aunt Martha in a spin for weeks."

"Let's do it, then."

She laughed, and he laughed with her, and her heart swelled with joy as her fears melted away. It would be all right. It would really be all right. She would marry Luke, and with the children they would be a family. Together they would face all the trials and happiness that life had to offer. And when she made mistakes or Luke did, they would ask God for forgiveness and try to do better. As Luke said, it was all anyone could do.

Epilogue

~C

One year later...

"I can help finishing setting up the chairs," Tanner offered. "I'm not tired."

Luke shook his head. "You heard your mother, son. Bedtime. I'll expect you up by five to feed the livestock."

"Ya, Dat." He turned to his mother. "Should I wake Justice then?"

Honor gave Tanner a good-night hug, still unable to believe how he'd shot up in the last year. "Leave your little brothers to sleep. Justice can tend the chickens after breakfast." She tousled his hair affectionately. "Our first worship service for our new church is a special day of thanksgiving and celebration. We'll need you to help look after the younger ones." Tanner nodded, and she hugged him again.

"Good night, son. Don't forget your prayers," Luke reminded.

"Ne, Dat, I won't." With a final grin, Tanner left the parlor.

Honor watched him go, a lump rising in her throat. "He's growing up on us. Not just in height, but he seems so much more mature."

"Ya," Luke agreed. "He is. It's what children do." He unfolded two more chairs and added them to the women's row. "Do you need any help in the kitchen for tomorrow's midday meal?"

"I don't think so. I just hope I've made enough chicken salad. I have plenty of yeast rolls, but I wouldn't want to run out of salad."

He chuckled. "It's just six families, counting Freeman's and ours. We aren't feeding half of Kent County, not yet. And everyone else is bringing food. We'll have plenty."

She used her broom to reach a cobweb on the ceiling in one corner of the parlor. This newly expanded room would be plenty large enough for their first worship service. "Do you think I was selfish not to sell any of my land? Would Green Meadows have come together sooner, if I did?"

Luke shook his head. "Everything is in God's plan. If you *had* agreed, I'd not have gone to that English neighbor and asked him to let us know if he wanted to move. And you see what came of that?"

She smiled at him. "I still have a hard time believing it."

The neighbor had wanted to move to South Carolina to be near his grandchildren, so Luke and Freeman were able to purchase the ninety-four acres. They'd divided that three ways and found three Amish families to settle, including Luke's cousin Raymond's. And Freeman and Katie had just sold one of their lots to a young Amish couple who wanted to build a house, so they would soon join the new church community. Zipporah's family would also be joining them.

"We have our church," Luke said, sliding a big stuffed easy chair into position for one of the elders. "And our bishop and preachers."

They'd asked Bishop Atlee from Seven Poplars to help choose their first church leaders. According to tradition, God's ministers were chosen by lottery. The names were placed in identical Bibles and one picked at random by a designated elder. Freeman's uncle Jehu would be their first bishop, with Freeman and one of the newcomers, Abel Byler, as preachers. Some might be surprised that their bishop would be a blind man, but they didn't know Jehu. He had committed passages, stories and proverbs to memory, and he was full of wisdom and compassion. His capable, work-worn hands would help to mold the new community. And, surprising everyone, Luke was to be the new deacon, responsible for seeing that the Ordnung was followed.

It was all Honor could do not to feel pride that her Luke was chosen and that he had been so instrumental in forming the new Amish community, which they'd decided to call Green Meadows.

"...the school," Luke said. "Honor, are you listening to me?"

She felt her cheeks grow warm. "*Ya... Ne*, I was thinking how God has blessed us with good friends and so many opportunities. And *ya*, I am thrilled that we will have our own school just across the meadow."

"Thanks to you," he said. "You donated the land."

"What's an acre to see our children educated close to home? It was you and our new neighbors who built it. Without you, Luke, none of this would have happened." Her smile was tender. "My life changed when you showed up at my door."

"It's a good thing you opened the door that day. I was afraid you were going to leave me in the rain."

She laughed as Luke put his arms around her and hugged her. Then he kissed her full on the mouth. "You know that I love you," he said.

She nodded, too full of emotion to speak.

"And I love our four children. You know that, too?"

"*Ya*, I do. And they know it, too."

He smiled down at her, his arms warm around her shoulders, the familiar male scent of him enveloping her in a loving embrace. "I love being a father. And I have the woman of my heart for my wife." His lips brushed hers again, and she reveled in the sweetness.

"And I love you, Luke Weaver."

"Good. I want you to tell me that every day for the rest of our lives together." He drew his thumb across her cheek. "We should get to bed. Morning comes early."

She smiled at him, tears of joy clouding her eyes, her heart so full of happiness that she could hardly breathe. "I know, but tomorrow's the Sabbath," she worried. "I won't be able to make more chicken salad in the morning. I'm thinking I should make another batch."

"We have enough chicken salad," he said, bending to pick her up in his arms and swing her in a circle.

She squealed and clung to him. "Put me down!" she cried.

"Look around you, woman," he said, turning in a circle with her in his arms. "Your house is shining like a new penny, your cupboards, refrigerator and freezers are full, and we're ready to host our first worship service." He kissed her again.

"Put me down," she repeated, laughing. "What if one of the children should hear us?"

"I won't put you down until you agree to go away with me," he said. "Our honeymoon. We never did get it. I think next week would be an excellent time to finally take it."

"How long?"

"Two weeks?" he bargained. "No children. I've already talked to Katie and she's agreed to watch all four for as long as we want. And Greta will be here to help her."

"One week," Honor countered. "But where are you taking me?"

"That will be a surprise. And my final offer is ten days. Take it or—"

"Or what?"

"Or we'll stand here all night and greet our guests with me all red eyed from lack of sleep and you wearing your third-best apron and your oldest head scarf."

Honor laughed. "Eight days. And you have to promise me that you'll not get your picture in the newspapers or rescue anybody from drowning on our honeymoon."

"Sold!" He kissed her one last time and then set her lightly on the floor. "I'll try my best, unless it's you who's in danger, and then…" He shrugged. "Now, turn out the lamps and come to bed. It will be daylight soon, and we have guests arriving."

"Whatever you say, husband."

He locked the door, she turned off the lights and they walked up the wide stairs, her hand in his, with light hearts and high hopes for the days and years to come.

* * * * *

Dear Reader,

It's been so nice to spend time with you. I'm happy to have been able to share Honor and Luke's story. This time, the Amish matchmaker really had her hands full, didn't she? When Luke showed up at Honor's door that very first day, I was afraid Honor wouldn't let him in! And then where would my story have gone?

Thank goodness Honor had such a steady head and opened that door. I think the moment she saw Luke again, she secretly saw the possibility of love and happiness. Once or twice, though, I was afraid those naughty boys would put an end to the romance before it really got going. I think the Lord guided Luke, though, don't you? And in the end, true love—God's and the love between Luke and Honor—brought the couple together.

I hope that you enjoyed Luke and Honor's journey in search of happiness. Keep an eye out for my new Amish series, set in Chestnut Grove, where a blended family is just beginning their new life together.

Wishing you peace and joy,
Emma Miller

COMING NEXT MONTH FROM
Love Inspired®

Available February 20, 2018

AN UNEXPECTED AMISH ROMANCE
The Amish Bachelors • by Patricia Davids

Mourning a broken engagement, Helen Zook flees to Bowman's Crossing. There she finds herself clashing with her new boss, Mark Bowman. Sparks fly. But with Mark soon returning to his hometown, is there any chance at a future together?

COURTING THE AMISH DOCTOR
Prodigal Daughters • by Mary Davis

Single doctor Kathleen Yoder returns to her Amish community knowing acceptance of her profession won't come easy—but at least she has the charming Noah Lambright on her side. Even as Kathleen comes to depend on Noah's support, she knows an Amish husband would never accept a doctor wife. Could Noah be the exception?

A FAMILY FOR EASTER
Rescue River • by Lee Tobin McClain

When Fiona Farmingham offers to rent her carriage house to single dad Eduardo Delgado after a fire at his home, he accepts. Having failed his deceased wife, he plans to keep their relationship strictly professional. But six rambunctious kids, one wily dog and Fiona's kind heart soon have him falling for the pretty widow.

HER ALASKAN COWBOY
Alaskan Grooms • by Belle Calhoune

Honor Prescott is shocked former sweetheart Joshua Ransom is back in Love, Alaska—and that he's selling his grandfather's ranch to a developer! As a wildlife conservationist, Honor is determined to stop that sale. But when the secret behind Joshua's departure is revealed, can she prevent herself from falling for the Alaskan cowboy once again?

FINALLY A BRIDE
Willow's Haven • by Renee Andrews

Disappointed by love, veterinarian Haley Calhoun decides her practice and her Adopt-an-Animal program are enough. Until she discovers the handsome widower who showed up at her clinic with an orphaned boy and his puppy will be her point of contact for the adoption program. Will working together give both of them a second chance at forever?

THEIR SECRET BABY BOND
Family Blessings • by Stephanie Dees

Mom-to-be Wynn Sheehan left her dream job in Washington, DC, after her heart was broken. When she becomes the caregiver for Latham Grant's grandfather, she's drawn once again to her long-ago boyfriend. But with her life now in shambles, is her happily-ever-after out of reach for good?

LOOK FOR THESE AND OTHER LOVE INSPIRED BOOKS WHEREVER BOOKS ARE SOLD, INCLUDING MOST BOOKSTORES, SUPERMARKETS, DISCOUNT STORES AND DRUGSTORES.

LICNM0218

Get 2 Free Books,

Plus 2 Free Gifts—

just for trying the

Reader Service!

Love Inspired®

Fresh off heartbreak, will Helen Zook find peace in Bowmans Corner…and love again with her new boss?

Read on for a sneak preview of
AN UNEXPECTED AMISH ROMANCE
by **Patricia Davids**,
available March 2018 from Love Inspired!

Mark Bowman lifted his straw hat off his face and sat up with a disgruntled sigh. Trying to sleep on a bus was hard enough, but the sound of muffled weeping coming from the seat behind him was making it impossible. He turned to look over his shoulder. The culprit was an Amish woman with her face buried in a large white handkerchief. She was alone.

"*Frauline*, are you all right?"

She glanced up and then turned her face to the window. "I'm fine."

It was dark outside. There was nothing to see except the occasional lights from the farms they passed. She dabbed her eyes and sniffled. She was a lovely woman. Her pale blond hair was tucked neatly beneath a gauzy, heart-shaped white *kapp*. He didn't recognize the style and wondered where she was from. "You don't sound fine."

"Maybe not yet, but I will be."

The defiance in her tone took him by surprise and reminded him of his six-year-old sister when she didn't get her way. Experience had taught him the best way to stop his sister's tears was to distract her. "I don't care much for bus rides. Makes me queasy in the stomach. How about you?"

"It doesn't bother me."

"Where are you headed?"

"To visit family." The woman's clipped reply said she wasn't interested in talking about it. He should have let it go at that, but he didn't.

"Then someone in your family must be ill. Or perhaps you are on your way to a funeral."

She frowned at him. "Why do you say that?"

"It's a reasonable assumption. You'd hardly be crying if you were on your way to a wedding."

Tears welled up in her eyes and spilled down her cheeks. With a strangled cry, she scrambled out of her seat and moved to one at the rear of the bus, effectively ending their conversation.

Confused, he stared at her. Somehow he'd made things worse, and he had no idea what he'd said that upset her so. He shook his head in bewilderment.

Looking for inspiration in tales
of hope, faith and heartfelt romance?

Check out **Love Inspired**® and
Love Inspired® **Suspense** books!

New books available every month!

CONNECT WITH US AT:

Harlequin.com/Community

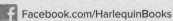